SHELFIE SABOTAGE

A SHELF INDULGENCE COZY MYSTERY

S.E. BABIN

OLIVER-HEBER BOOKS

Shelfie Sabotage Copyright 2024 © S.E. Babin

Cover art by Lou Harper from Cover Affairs

Published by Oliver-Heber Books

0 9 8 7 6 5 4 3 2 1

ONE

My to-do list was as frightening as the bag of Halloween decorations Harper had hauled in this morning and scattered across the floor to sift through. October blew in like a lion, shifting most of the landscape to a stunning array of orange and reds. Driving to work, while never a hassle, had become a pleasure every day I drove past all the gorgeous fall foliage.

October meant Halloween and tourists driving in to gawk at the seasonal color change. It also meant Harper went nuts at the craft store for the annual Silverwood Hollow window display contest. It had a more official title, but it was a decorating contest for everyone who wanted to participate. The top prize was a spread in The Gazette, a trophy, five hundred bucks, and a gift certificate to the top steakhouse in the closest large city, a place I rarely made it out to. I always participated, but Harper had become the brains surrounding the theme, as well as the person I handed my checkbook to and commanded her to make it happen.

She did so happily, but I was beginning to wonder if maybe I should set a budget next time. Tattered Pages looked like Halloween had thrown up all over the floor.

At my look of dismay, Harper laughed and held up her hands. "It's going to be amazing, I promise."

"I don't doubt it, but does the store have any decorations left?" Piles of plastic bones, squirmy spiders, dozens of bags of fake spiderwebs, and miscellaneous fall and Halloween decor made the store look less like a bookshop and more like someone had stumbled into a macabre, confusing crime scene with us as the culprits.

Harper waved my words away. "I had to arrive early to get the good stuff." Her eyes glittered with the thrill of the hunt. "Plus, I drove all the way to the Home Goods store because I heard they put out their new decor this morning." She rubbed her hands together gleefully. "We're going to crush our competition."

"I've created a monster," I murmured.

She snickered. "I don't want that Jack guy to win. Last year, he had that really cool display with the lights and music, so we have to one-up him this time."

My brows lifted. "Music?"

She nodded, cheeks flushed with the weather and the possibility of winning.

"If you think I'm listening to The Monster Mash on repeat for the next thirty days, you're insane."

"What if it's the only thing between us and first place?" She stuck her bottom lip out in a pout.

"I'm afraid my sanity will have to settle for second place," I said dryly. "Show me your plan. Minus the music."

Harper clapped her hands together and rattled off her idea. By the time she finished, I was both in awe of her creativity and a little rattled by her single-minded determination to win at all costs.

Jack owned a furniture shop at the edge of the downtown strip. It was relatively new to the area—opened less than a year ago. I wondered how a furniture store would survive in an area ruled by tourism, but then I peeked in his shop window and found myself drooling over some of his pieces. I later found out he handmade everything in the wood shop on his land.

He was pretty easy on the eyes, too. Of course, my guy was way easier on the eyes, so my observation was purely clinical.

Harper had spoken about him a few times before, and it was unusual for her, so I started paying attention. I didn't want to tease her about it, but I suspected there was more under the surface to this obsession over Jack winning the window display competition.

She'd dated a few people over the last year, but none had lasted. I never probed. It wasn't my business, but Harper was my friend, and the only thing I wanted for her was happiness.

"I have a date tonight," she said out of the blue.

Speaking of...was it Jack? "Who's the lucky guy?"

Harper shrugged. "I met him at speed dating."

A bark of laughter escaped before I slapped my hand over my mouth.

She rolled her eyes, but a rueful smile curved her lips up. "It's hard being single in a small town. You got lucky. Hardy only had eyes for you right away."

She was right. I was lucky. Hardy and I had a rocky start and an even rockier middle, but we'd managed to right the boat, and since then, things had been smooth sailing.

"I think it's a matter of meeting the right person at the right time," I said gently. "You're amazing. You'll find someone."

She snorted. "Hopefully soon. It's awkward attending events around here. There aren't many singles, and those who are left aren't exactly my type."

I reached over and squeezed her arm. "I promise. You'll find someone."

She would. I knew it. And maybe I'd speed that along by asking Hardy if he had any single friends. We didn't often see police officers around. Silverwood Hollow was mostly safe. I saw the police way more than Harper did because of my investigative work now and before I was licensed.

Now that Hardy and I were engaged, I had the paper-work ready to change the name of my P.I. firm to Cavanaugh Investigations, but I was holding off until we officially tied the knot. I wasn't worried, but life had a way of complicating things when one least expected it.

Speaking of...

The bell jingled, revealing my fiancé and my soon-to-be stepdaughter.

"Dakota!" Izzy cried, hurtling across the room like a rocket.

I opened my arms, and she launched herself at me. Catching her with an *oof* of expelled air, I laughed. Her strawberry shampoo slammed into my nose, along with a ton of dark hair.

"Izzy," Hardy said in exasperation. "Dakota's not as big as I am. Be careful about tackling her."

Izzy giggled. "She caught me!"

I caught his eye over the top of Izzy's shoulder. His gaze softened. "Hey." He walked over and dropped a kiss on top of my head.

"Hi."

Hardy ruffled Izzy's hair before his attention turned to the explosion of Halloween decorations around us. "We came at just the right time."

I laughed. Izzy would love helping us. "Harper is competing against the furniture maker down the road."

"Jack?" he asked.

I nodded.

"Yes," Harper grumbled. "He went way over the top last year, so I have to make sure he doesn't beat us this time."

"I can see that," Hardy said dryly, his attention snagging on a tangle of glow in the dark skeleton lights.

Izzy pulled away from the hug and gasped as she

finally noticed the decorations. "Oooh," she whispered. "You're decorating the store?"

"Mostly the window," I said.

"But a few of the tables," Harper interjected. She held her hand out to Izzy. "Want to help?"

Izzy scrambled out of my lap and let Harper help her up. Harper winked as she led Izzy away, chatting about the different kinds of decorations she'd bought.

Hardy helped me up and pulled me close for a kiss, his cold nose brushing against my cheek when he pulled away. I'd never get tired of his kisses.

The bell over the door rang again.

"Gross," Daniel Jensen said good-naturedly, as he walked in holding three coffees.

Hardy laughed. "Jealous?"

"Always," Daniel grumbled.

I'm glad those two had hashed out whatever macho thing they had going on. They were still a little antago-nistic toward each other, but it was mainly in a competitive way now and not angry anymore. We'd once again settled into an odd friendship, but this time it felt more secure than it ever was.

After the last case, Daniel and I had tiptoed around each other for a while. I'd found out way more about him than I ever wanted to know, and he had relinquished more about his life than he ever wanted to. When it was over, I realized I had no right to judge Daniel for his decisions or lack thereof because he'd never treated me poorly or given me any reason to distrust him.

Plus, I'd chosen Hardy, and there was never a chance there'd be anything more between us. It took Daniel a little longer to accept that, but once he had, we'd fallen back into an easy rhythm, but Hardy came to chess nights now.

Speaking of chess, Hardy insisted he was very close to figuring out how Daniel was cheating on the game. Daniel, however, continued to insist he was a savant.

He handed me a coffee first, then Hardy, and I motioned for them to head back into the new office. With all the decorations spread out everywhere, walking around the bookshop felt like navigating a maze.

The smell of lavender and Earl Grey floated up. "London Fog?"

"Yup. Half sugar, as you prefer."

"Stop trying to steal my girl," Hardy grumbled.

"I got you black," Daniel responded. "Like your soul."

I snorted and sank onto the loveseat. The newest part of Tattered Pages was finally finished. A clear glass door separated the P.I. agency from the rest of the store, but I'd kept the bookish theme running through the entire space.

Hardy left the force a couple of months ago, about eight months after our engagement. We'd been slow to act on wedding plans, not because we didn't want to get married, but because we wanted Izzy, Hardy's daughter, to fully settle in and get used to all the changes around her.

She'd lost her home and her mom, started a new school, and had to adjust to a dad she'd never met before. All those changes would have been difficult for an adult. I couldn't imagine what it was like for a seven-year-old. Izzy and I got along like peanut butter and jelly, but I treaded carefully when it came to acting like her mom. I wanted to be her mom, but I knew there would always be a void in her heart for her biological mom, Hardy's former fiancée, and the woman who'd signed away her rights.

The entire situation broke my heart, but I never brought it up unless Hardy or Izzy wanted to talk about it. I let Izzy lead the way, and I straddled the line between being her friend and an adult who set and enforced rules. To be honest, I had no idea how to be a mom. I guess no one did until parenthood was thrust upon them. I leaned on Mom and Gran as much as I could.

But...both of those women spoiled Izzy like she was the queen of the world, something that exasperated me and Hardy to no end, but it was mostly harmless. Both were careful not to spoil her too much, but a couple of times, they went a little overboard and we had to gently correct the ship.

Izzy, to Mom and Gran's great delight, had nicknames for both. Mom was Gigi, and Gran was Nana. No idea how either one of those came to be, but Izzy was happy, and that was all that mattered.

As much as I wanted to rush to the altar, waiting was the right thing to do. Watching Izzy bloom had only solidified it. The day we received the final paperwork severing Izzy's biological mother's parental rights was a hard day. I'd quietly left the house and let Hardy speak to Izzy. I hadn't been gone twenty minutes when Hardy asked me to come back.

The moment I stepped inside the house, Izzy launched herself in my arms and cried for the next two hours. We had plans to go to the skating rink that night, but instead, we ordered pizza and stayed in, watching movies.

Things were much different now. Izzy was happier, more adjusted, and ready for Hardy and me to walk down the aisle. As amazing as that was, it meant we had to plan a wedding.

Which brought us to today, back in my office, next to a desk scattered with a dozen wedding catalogs and pressure to set a date.

Daniel took a sip of his coffee and smirked when he spotted the catalogs. "Still no date?"

"Not yet. You'll be at the dinner?" I asked.

"Wouldn't miss it for the world. Mind if I bring a date?"

I grinned. "Did you meet her at a signing?"

Hardy snickered.

"I long for the day that joke will get old," Daniel said with a sigh. "And no, she's not from a signing. She's a fellow author."

I leaned forward with interest. "Who? What does she write? Is she interested in doing a signing?"

Daniel laughed and waved me away. "I'm not telling you anything, Nosy Nellie."

I gasped in mock outrage. "I will not apologize for trying to keep the citizens of Silverwood Hollow entertained by bringing them the best literary talent in the state!"

Daniel rolled his eyes. "Sure you are. She likes attention less than I do. Plus, she doesn't live in the state."

"Oooh. Long distance? How's that going?"

"Hardy," Daniel said, a note of exasperation in his voice. "Call your guard dog off."

My fiancé laughed. "Have you met Dakota? There's no help for you once she sinks her teeth in."

"Har har," I said. A knock on the door surprised us all.

A head full of red hair popped in. "Am I interrupting?"

"Hey!"

Fletcher O'Day, stunning redhead, reporter at the local Gazette, and a new friend of mine, grinned. "I'm here to see if you're free for lunch tomorrow. I want to go over some of the catering notes for the dinner."

"Ugh," I said.

Fletcher laughed. "This is just the dinner. We haven't gotten to the wedding yet."

"I know." Rubbing a hand over my face, I motioned her in with the other. "Want to chat for a minute?"

Fletcher lowered herself into the chair across from me. "Are you sure you don't need me to do anything else? I'm happy to help."

"Catering is more than enough. Thanks again for offering." Planning anything was a massive pain, but I had no idea how difficult it was to plan anything like a wedding. Fletcher was right. A lot of those wedding catalogs had checklists inside, and the thought of getting all that done in a timely manner made my head explode.

I'd already booked a local restaurant for the dinner, but

Fletcher was working with the chef to come up with a special dinner for all the guests. Five courses—two meat and a vegetarian option—four choices for an appetizer, then salad, and four dessert choices, with a final option for coffee or cappuccino.

Out of fifty invites sent, we had thirty-five people who responded *yes*. I left my card on file with the restaurant and told Fletcher there was no budget. She'd given me the side-eye over that one and asked me if I was a closet Bridezilla.

I wasn't. Hardy and I were stupid rich; we just hadn't told anyone.

Neither one of us was too interested in being murdered, so we kept tidbits like that to ourselves.

I told her Mom and Gran were helping and that we had a lot of leeway with the cost. Neither of us wanted a huge wedding. If it were up to us, we'd run down to the City Hall and take care of it. But Mom and Gran lost their mind when I mentioned it, and Izzy already had no less than ten flower-girl dresses picked out.

So we decided to put most of the money into the engagement dinner and reception but also have a nice, but short, wedding at the local non-denominational church in town.

It'd been a long while since this town had a big celebration, and neither one of us had an issue with throwing a party.

We just had to get through the engagement dinner first.

So far, though, all I had was the restaurant booked. No decorations, no music, no outfit, not much of anything planned, except for the menu—which Fletcher was navigating for us.

"We'll run through everything tomorrow. Hardy, you interested in coming?"

Hardy looked at me. "Want me to be there?"

I shrugged. "Do you have an opinion on the menu?"

He grunted. "Steak for one of the meat choices. Other than that, the sky's the limit."

"Alright, then. Looks like it's just you and me," I said to Fletcher.

"Oh," Hardy added. "Izzy would like key lime pie as one of the dessert options."

I laughed. "During fall?"

Hardy shrugged. "You know how reasonable a seven-year-old is."

Fletcher grinned and took her notebook and pen out. "I'll see what I can do. Does she have a second choice?"

Hardy thought about it. "She'll forgive you for the lack of key lime if chocolate is involved."

Fletcher made an additional note. "That is definitely doable." She tucked the pen and pad back into her purse and rose. "One o'clock, okay?" she asked.

I pulled out my phone and checked my schedule. "Good with me. Two martini limit?"

Fletcher laughed. "Depends on how much down the rabbit hole we go with planning. I got Hardy's number. I'll call him if he needs to pick you up."

Hardy grinned. "She can have the day off if it gets that bad."

I shook my head. "A girl goes out for martinis one time..."

Fletcher gave a cheery wave and breezed out.

"I like her," Daniel said.

"She's way too normal for you," Hardy quipped.

I covered my mouth to hide my grin.

"Plus, Cole is in love with her," I said, when the danger of laughing passed. "And I think she's halfway there."

Hardy's eyebrows rose. "Fletcher is getting on board?"

"She's making him work for it, at least," I said. "He hasn't been on a date since that restaurant."

Daniel laughed when Hardy's cheeks went pink. He'd gone out with one of Cole's coworkers, a lively woman named Charlotte. When Hardy had spotted me on a fake date with Daniel, he'd lost his cool in front of Charlotte, ruining any chance of romance between them. It worked out for the best, as neither of us really wanted to date anyone else, but it was a rocky road for a while.

I gracefully changed the subject, not missing Hardy's look of thanks. "How's the deadline coming?" I asked Daniel.

"It's going." He shook his head. "After this many books, I'm having to get a lot more creative about murdering someone."

"You should try plants. Lots of ways to kill someone with the local flora."

Hardy and Daniel gave me weird looks. "Is that right?" my fiancé asked.

I gave them an innocent smile. "It is. Plus, it's sneaky."

"It's a woman's way to murder," Daniel added. "I haven't had a female serial killer yet. Maybe I could make her a botany professor." I could see the wheels turning in his head.

"Yes!" I exclaimed. "But you can't do it for this one, right? Aren't you too far in?"

He shrugged. "I am, but that's a great idea for a series." Just like Fletcher, he magically produced a little notebook and pen and jotted some notes down.

"If you really want to skid off the rails, you could make it magical."

He waved the pen at me before he put it back into his pocket. "No. I get paid to be Daniel Jensen, the guy who kills people who deserve it, sans magic."

"Maybe you could take a pen name and write a riveting thriller series about a network of botany professors who belong to a coven of generational witches sworn to protect all womankind."

There was a long silence. Daniel cursed under his breath, pulled the notepad and pen out, and jotted something else down.

I fist-pumped the air. "Ha! I expect a dedication."

Daniel sighed and rose, tossing his empty coffee cup into the trash. "You truly are a thorn in my side, Dakota."

Hardy laughed.

"A thorn who just made you a million bucks!" I called to his retreating form.

When we heard the door jingle, Hardy rose and tugged me to a standing position, circling my waist with his arms. "I'm going to check our e-mails and see if we have any new requests."

We'd had a few small cases since Daniel's, but it wasn't as busy as I expected. It wasn't a big deal, and Hardy assured me it was nothing to worry about. Those kinds of agencies were difficult to get off the ground, he said, and it would take a while before people realized exactly what we did.

Opening the place had been a gamble, but I'd proven quite good at solving cases. My stats were even better with Hardy around. He'd given me a lot of ideas on marketing and how to get the word out about what we did. To keep himself busy while we got the business off the ground, he occasionally moonlighted as a consultant for the police department.

The paycheck he received for his first gig had enraged him. "You mean I could have been paid this much the entire time?"

"Consultants always make more money," I'd told him.

"Yes, well, maybe I should have quit a long time ago and offered my services as a consultant," he grumbled.

Hardy dropped a kiss on my lips and headed out of the office. I tossed my cup in the trash and went to the desk, sweeping my hands over the wedding catalogs.

A four-tiered cake caught my eye. I tugged the catalog out and ran my fingers over the glossy page. The icing was a pristine white, decorated with a riot of colorful sugar flowers and tiny, iridescent pearls.

Trudy could have made this. Grief speared my heart every time I thought of her. Her absence had affected everyone in town. People came from hours away to delight in her baked goods, and I'd been the one to discover what she'd been up to, resulting in her selling her restaurant. I'd bought the property, and I'm afraid it didn't exactly endear me to the townsfolk.

In my defense, our properties backed up to each other. Buying the restaurant was the perfect way to expand the shop, and I didn't think I should have to apologize for it. I wasn't the one who broke the law, but I was the one who discovered it. I can see how it might look bad to those who might not know me or exactly what happened, but as much as I missed her and her delightful creations, turning over the evidence was the right thing to do.

I flipped through the pages until I found the cake, skimming down the page until I located the baker. New York.

A huff of breath escaped me. Way too far away to hire. I tore the page out and folded it into four before tucking it into my pocket.

Maybe Fletcher would know a baker. She had a ton of connections within and outside of town. If anyone could help me find someone who could make it, she could.

This is how they get you, I thought, as I headed back into the bookstore.

I could feel the money in my bank account disappearing in an explosion of sugar, lace, and tablecloths.

TWO

Hardy and Izzy had left by the time I walked out. Something must have come up. I lamented being unable to say goodbye, but I'd see them later this evening. Harper grinned as she scooped up the last of the decorations. They'd started part of the window display, mostly the fall leaf-covered ground, made out of pretty brown fabric and fall-themed leaf and pinecone confetti.

Harper had a weird fascination with themed hole punchers. The woman could make seasonal confetti like no one's business. If she hadn't seemed happy here, I'd wonder if her second calling was flooding the world with weird confetti patterns.

"There's still so much to do!" she sang, as she tied the bag shut and stuck it inside a larger brown paper bag.

"Have you seen what Jack is doing yet?"

She clicked her tongue. "He covered up the window!" Her voice quivered with outrage.

I bit my smile down.

"Can you believe that?" Harper rolled her eyes and grabbed the broom, sweeping up random bits of confetti and trash.

"Considering you've been stalking his window display? Yes, I can believe that."

Harper snorted and tapped the almost full dustpan against the top of the trash can. "All's fair in love and war..."

"I don't see any love in this scenario," I said dryly.

Harper clipped the dustpan to the broom and returned it to the corner. "Love of decorating. Winning." She flashed a grin as she grabbed the bag of decorations and put it back behind the register. "You good with Izzy coming by tomorrow to help again?"

"If she's interested in helping, she's always welcome." Izzy hung around the bookstore more and more these days. She was a quiet but curious child. While her nose was usually in a book when she stayed here, there were days when she'd come in full of questions, some of which I had no idea how to answer. Thankfully, they were all innocent questions–the type I could open a book and find the answers to.

"Awesome. She's a great kid."

I smiled, my heart warming at the words. "Yeah. She really is."

Harper hesitated. "How's she doing? With everything?"

'Everything' meant her mother signing her rights over.

I lifted a shoulder in a shrug. "Hardy has her in therapy. I think it's helping, but there's no way to ever fill that hole. Hopefully, we can help her patch it, though."

"Well, I'm always available for babysitting duty."

"Hardy has some family scattered around who are always ready and willing, but if she ever wants a sleepover with Auntie Harper, I'll be sure to call you."

Harper's cheeks went pink. Izzy had started calling her Auntie a few months ago, and it stuck. None of us corrected her, especially not Harper. She loved being an auntie and spent a lot of time with Izzy when she came into the store. It hadn't moved beyond store visits, but I'm sure it would in time.

I jerked my chin to the window. "What's next?"

Harper's eyes glittered. "We build the Halloween village, add the smoke machine and lights, and put the music on a motion timer."

I winced. "Smoke machine?"

Harper laughed. "Yeah. We're going to put little pink and purple lights to color the smoke. It's going to be amazing by the time we're finished."

I threw my hands in the air. "I give up!"

"About time," Harper said. "It's decorating season, Dakota. Ninety percent of the people in this town become monsters when it comes to fall decor."

My phone dinged with a text.

We got a case!

Relief filled me. Hardy was great at checking out the details of any potential case before we took it on. If he'd gotten back to me this quickly, it meant he'd found something worth it and not too difficult. If something looked too out of our wheelhouse, he'd refer it to someone else, though that had occurred only once since we began working together.

Awesome. I'll swing by the house in a couple of hours. Harper and I still have some inventory to sort through.

I'll be here. Love you.

Even though I responded with a heart emoji, it would never encompass how I felt about him.

With my heart full, I turned my attention back to Harper. "Ready to finish inventory?"

Harper's groan had me chuckling all the way back to the office.

I PULLED into Hardy's driveway—no, *our* driveway now —and let myself inside the house. So much had changed over the last few months. I'd given up my home to move in here so as not to disrupt Izzy anymore. His house was larger than mine and had more room, plus he had some land and room to expand. We decided to stay here for a while—at least until we got married—and start looking at another property with additional land to spread out.

Although we'd talked about moving in together, we hesitated until Izzy started complaining about going back and forth to my house and theirs all the time. We sat her down and talked about it, only to realize she was ecstatic about the possibility of me being there all the time.

This felt like a dream I might wake up from any day now, and I had to pinch myself each day and remind myself this was my new reality.

Hardy sat at the kitchen table, a pair of readers perched on the tip of his nose. I grinned at the sight and slid a hand through his hair. He snagged me around the waist and tipped me onto his lap.

My cry of surprise made him chuckle into my neck.

"Hi." His breath was warm against my collarbone.

"Where's Izzy?"

"Homework." Hardy nuzzled the sensitive spot between my neck and shoulder.

Goosebumps raced down my arms. "So we can make out a little?"

Hardy snorted. "A little. Not too much funny business."

I wrapped my arms around his neck and pressed my lips against his. "Maybe a little funny business," I murmured.

THREE

By the time Izzy came out of her room, Hardy and I were focused on next month's calendar. On the first day of every month, we sat down and planned out the next month, so we were always thirty days ahead.

Izzy's face brightened when she saw me. I gave her a one-armed hug and a kiss on the cheek. "Want some lunch?"

"Grilled cheese?" she asked hopefully.

I pretended to think about it. "I was thinking broccoli and Brussels sprouts."

Her nose wrinkled. "Pancakes?"

"Mmm. What about liver and onions?"

Izzy made a gagging noise. "Gross!"

"It's very good for your blood."

Izzy held out her arm and studied it. "My blood doesn't need any more goodness."

Hardy chuckled as I rose. "Fine then," I said. "Blue cheese and onion grilled cheese?"

"Dakoooootaaaaa," Izzy moaned.

I let out a long-suffering sigh. "Fine. Fine. American ooey gooey cheese it is."

Izzy clapped her hands.

"With lots of onions," I added.

"Daaaaaad!"

Hardy grinned at us both. "I'll take your onions, I guess."

Izzy peered at me.

I shrugged. "I suppose that's all right."

Fifteen minutes later, a stack of grilled cheese sat at the table. Izzy launched herself at it, taking a huge bite out of the first one. This kid could seriously eat. She never took more than she could handle, but most kids I knew barely finished any of their food. Izzy would finish both sandwiches and ask for more if she were still hungry.

We chatted as we munched on sandwiches and chips. Hardy's phone went off a couple of times, but he ignored it, as did I. The new household had strict phone rules set by both of us. No phones at the table. No phones after six p.m. We'd set our voice-mails to tell people we wouldn't answer after that time, but to call the house phone if there were an emergency. The house phone was relatively new, and only a handful of people had the number.

Hardy had set up special ringtones for certain people. He'd answer them if they called after six. I had it set up for

Mom, Gran, and Harper, but everyone was getting used to the new rules.

It gave us a much-needed data break, and allowed us to keep our attention on Izzy and the here and now.

"We need two good cases to make a profit next month," Hardy said in between bites.

"Nothing on the books yet?" I asked.

"Not yet, but I've left business cards around the area and let everyone know I'm fully on board with you now."

It was a good thing. Hardy was an excellent detective. If they hesitated to hire me based on my background, Hardy's might convince them. He'd admitted to me it was unfair, especially since I was instrumental in solving multiple cases around town, but we couldn't change people's minds, could we?

I suspected it had something to do with Trudy shutting down her shop, but Hardy insisted that wasn't the reason. Either way, we were still doing well enough to keep going, and that's all that mattered.

Daniel also recommended our services to anyone he could. P.I. services were a niche market, and it's not like we sold a product. We sold services, and most people would never need us more than once.

My head jerked up. "What if we could contract with local businesses?"

Hardy's brow furrowed. "Like what?"

I waved my sandwich around, making Izzy giggle. "Like insurance companies or companies who need to investigate workplace accidents."

His expression cleared and turned thoughtful. "I don't know why I didn't think of that."

"You think it's viable?" I asked, my hopes lifting.

"More than viable." He wiped his hands on a napkin and typed something up on his laptop. "We'll need to make a list of anyone we can approach and set appointments with them."

"Maybe we can reach out to Cole, too."

Hardy nodded. "Reporters are natural investigators, but there might be some stories they need more discretion with. Good idea."

We smiled at each other and finished our lunch.

I'd successfully come up with an idea to add more income to the business and also procrastinated on the engagement dinner.

Multi-tasking, Dakota is thy name.

Harper called a few hours later.

"Everything okay?" I greeted.

She snorted. "Yes. Everything is fine. I'm calling because you haven't said much about your engagement dinner."

"It's still on, if that's what you're asking."

Harper laughed. "I know that, but I know how you feel about planning certain things. I'm calling to ask you if you want me to take that over?"

Oh gosh. Yes. Yes, I would, but I couldn't say yes. Maybe I could do the Irish thing, where she'd ask me twice and I'd demur, but pounce when she asked me the third time.

Granted, this was very different and a lot more work than putting on a kettle of water for tea, but Harper loved planning things. I'd rather faceplant into a mud puddle and hide than plan a party.

I planned signings all the time, but I felt like those were different. It was work and it should feel like work, so those didn't bother me as much.

An engagement party was for me, and therefore, planning it gave me the hives.

"I couldn't possibly ask you to do that," I said.

"You aren't asking me! I'm asking *you*!"

"That's far too much work to put on your plate. You still have to decorate the window!"

Harper let out an exasperated breath. "It's a window, Dakota. And it's fun! I'm asking you because I know how much you hate planning things for yourself. So I'll ask again. Do you want me to take this over?"

"There isn't too much left to do," I insisted. "Fletcher has the catering taken care of—"

Harper gasped. "Fletcher! You asked *Fletcher* instead of me?"

"Whoa. No, I did not. Fletcher insisted."

"Then I'm insisting!" she growled. "I know you don't want to do this."

I felt about two feet tall. "I don't," I admitted.

Hardy barked a laugh from the couch. I shot him a glare, which only made his grin widen. He knew how much I hated this, too. He'd stepped up and taken care of the invitations, but there were still a million things left to do.

"Then I insist," Harper declared, in the bossy tone that got her hired and made me pay her better than any other bookstore worker in the state. "I'll stop by tonight to pick everything up. Leave me notes about what you want, and I'll do my best to ensure it happens."

"I just want everyone to be fed," I admitted.

I could imagine Harper's look of horror. There was a long silence before Harper let out a long sigh. "Even if you told me *no*, I'd take this over after that remark. Seven p.m. I'll be there. Have everything ready."

She didn't let me say goodbye before she disconnected.

Dang. If I was this whiny over an engagement dinner, maybe I needed to hire someone to help with the rest.

I put my phone on the table and gave Hardy a sheepish look. He burst out laughing.

"Maybe it's time we hire a wedding planner?" he asked.

FOUR

Several days went by, the time passing like a blur to me. Harper and Izzy had worked hard on the window display, and I had to admit, it was impressive.

Annoying but impressive.

After hearing The Monster Mash several times an hour all day long, I finally made them turn off the motion detector. Now, if they wanted to hear the music, someone had to push the button manually.

Something Izzy did with wild abandon.

We received a lot more walk-in traffic due to the display, something I needed to keep in mind once October was over. I'd done window displays before, but I slacked off once the store got busier. If it brought in as much money as it had been over the last few days, I'd happily shell out for as many decorations as we needed to keep the themes going all year round.

Harper was beside herself with glee and had already

started a budget spreadsheet to calculate how much she'd need in funds over the year. She gave Izzy access to the list portion of the sheet and showed her how to add things she liked to it.

Just like my mom and grandma had created a monster, Harper teaching Izzy how to browse online for decor led her to become a Pinterest expert in no time flat.

Hardy took this new development in stride, saying at least it was better than that other app all the kids were using.

Harper and I sat on the couches, taking a break once the traffic died down. I snapped my fingers. "How'd the date go? I forgot to ask!"

Harper blushed. "Really good. We've been on a few more since then."

I blinked in surprise. "Wow. You must like him."

"I do. He's talking about becoming official."

My eyebrows rose. "Are you ready for that?" I noticed she didn't use the word *we*. *He's* talking about becoming official. Not *we*. Interesting.

She shrugged. "He's handsome, kind, chivalrous..." Her voice trailed off when she saw my look. "Don't worry. I haven't fallen in love."

I chuckled nervously. "It's happening fast. Sometimes it goes that way. I just want you to be careful."

"I will. He's somewhat new to town, and looking for a place to buy."

Dread pooled in my stomach. "Oh? Where's he staying?"

Harper blushed again. "With me for a few days."

Oh, Harper. There was a term for men like this.

Hobosexual.

It meant a man who moved lightning fast in relation-ships, pretending to be in love because they needed a place to stay.

"Ah," I said because, honestly, it was all I could say. Harper was a grown woman entitled to make her own decisions.

"I know," Harper groaned. "It's only for a few days. He has some appointments with a local realtor, and once he signs the contract, he's going to ask for a quick close."

"Maybe more than a few days?" I asked.

She shrugged. "I dunno. It's nice having a man around."

I smiled and let it go. This was absolutely none of my business. Being nosy solved a lot of cases, but Harper wasn't a case. She was my friend and my employee. This wasn't my circus. "I hope it works out."

She chuckled. "I can see your reservation written all over your face, but I appreciate your restraint."

I winced and gave her a sheepish look. "Sorry. The only time being nosy benefits me is when it involves a case." A sigh escaped me. "If you need anything at all, call me. You're more than an employee to me, Harper. I hope you know that."

Tears filled her eyes. She cleared her throat and looked away. "Thanks, Dakota. Everything is fine, but I'll remember that."

"Good." I patted her on the arm and grabbed my purse from under the register. "I'm headed out. Hardy and I have a stakeout." I wiggled my eyebrows at her.

She snorted and shook her head. "I can't believe that's not even the weirdest thing I've ever heard you say."

I laughed all the way to my car.

THE ONLY OTHER stakeout I'd been involved in was with Cole and Fletcher, who bickered almost the entire time. In spite of that, I still had a lot of fun.

Hardy proved to be a much more intense stakeout partner than those two. He frowned at my bag of snacks and grumbled that I was going to have to pee if I brought a thermos of coffee.

In response, I waved the thermos under his nose. "You shall pry my coffee from my cold, dead fingers."

Hardy snorted. "You're going to have to pee in a ditch."

"Hardy!"

"Them's the stakeout rules. Coffee is a diuretic. We may be in a spot with no bathrooms around. If you have to pee, you're going to have to go behind the car or into a ditch."

"If you make me pee in a ditch, the wedding is off," I groused.

Hardy grinned at me. "They make this thing you can strap around your waist and hook to your underwear, so you can pee while you're sitting."

I could almost see the steam coming out of my ears. "You want me to pee my pants?"

"No. You pee in the tube."

"That's located in my pants."

Hardy shrugged. "I'll add one to my shopping cart later."

I exhaled a huff of air. "Fine," I growled, setting the thermos down on the table. "Cole is way more fun to go on stakeouts with than you are."

One of his eyebrows rose. He stepped into my personal space. "You forget that during downtimes, you and I can make out. Can you and Cole do that?"

I pretended to think about it.

Hardy snorted and tugged on a loose strand of hair. "The answer to that question had better always be *no*."

"I mean, I could, I suppose. He seemed way more into the redhead than me, though."

Hardy grabbed the tote bag of snacks and tossed it over his shoulder. "Good. Fletcher is a good match for him. She won't put up with his shenanigans."

"Probably because Fletcher is way more full of shenanigans than he is."

He didn't know Fletcher as well as I did, but he'd been involved in a couple of calls involving the people she was investigating, some that came a little too close to restraining-order territory. Hardy grunted with amusement. "Dress warm. We'll need to keep the engine off."

He wore a pair of blue jeans, black boots, and a charcoal wool sweater, with a dark scarf wrapped around his neck.

Yummy.

I looked down at myself and frowned. "This isn't good enough?"

"Your pants are too thin, and you're wearing flats. I have some extra long johns if you want to put them on underneath, but I'd suggest switching to heavier denim, wool socks, and boots."

I stretched up and planted a kiss on his lips. "I never realized how bossy you are."

He put his hands on my shoulders, turned me, and marched me back to the bedroom. "I'll help you."

I grinned and let him steer me.

FIVE

Our new case was marital—my least favorite. I didn't like seeing this side of Silverwood Hollow. Hardy disliked them just as much as I did, but he was more willing to take them on. As a police officer, he saw the worst of people every single day.

Thankfully, I didn't know this couple. The woman had sent us a desperate message through our website, asking us for surveillance on her husband of twenty-five years. She noticed a marked change in his behavior about three months ago. The usual things—hiding his phone, deleting messages, going to the gym after years of neglect...

"Maybe there's a good explanation," I said lamely, wishing I'd brought my thermos.

Hardy reached over and entwined his fingers in mine. "Maybe."

Mr. Monroe stumbled out of the local watering hole in

the next town over, his arm around a short bottle-blonde with frizzy hair and too-bright lipstick.

"Maybe not," I grumbled.

We watched grimly as the man and woman headed toward the parking lot, laughing too loud, their hands roaming all over each other. Hardy lifted the camera, the rapid-fire click of the shutter sounding like gunfire in the silent car.

"If I weren't already judging him for infidelity, I'd definitely judge him for drinking and driving." We watched him open the passenger door and pour the woman in before he wobbled over to the driver's side.

"Should I call it in?" I asked.

"Not yet. The roads are empty tonight. If he gets into a dangerous spot, I'll stop him. We need to see where he's going."

I frowned.

"Don't worry. I contacted a friend of mine in the department. He knows where we are. We don't need anything official on the record if we want to keep our reputation for discretion."

Hardy thought of everything. "Well. Can we stop for coffee on the way home, then?"

He shook his head and started the car.

Mr. Monroe swerved all the way to an apartment complex two miles down the road. Fortunately for him, the only other soul on the road was us. I yawned and turned the heater down.

"I won't be able to stay awake if I get any warmer."

"Need me to put the window down?"

"No. It's okay. We shouldn't be too much longer, I hope?"

"I don't think so. This is obviously not his apartment. Let me get a few more pictures, and we should be able to put this to bed."

I tugged my cardigan closer and took the camera from the top of the dashboard.

The couple got out just as handsy as before, but this time, I was able to get dozens of shots that proved those two were way more than just friends. Every click of the shutter hurt my heart a little bit more. Tonight, we'd break a woman's heart.

But I hoped once the initial hurt passed, we helped set her free.

HARDY OFFERED to meet with the woman the next morning, but we were a team, so we went together.

We met outside of Silverwood Hollow at a small coffee shop I'd never been to before. Like most coffee shops, this one smelled heavenly. A large warehouse outside the place boasted a sign letting everyone know they roasted their own beans.

"How many pounds of coffee do you think they store in there?" I asked, as we got out of the car.

Hardy sent me an amused look. "It always goes back to the coffee with you."

I shrugged. "I never claimed to be unpredictable."

Hardy inhaled. "This place smells amazing."

"I hope anyone who lives close by likes coffee. Can you imagine waking up to this every day?" I took a deep breath. "Heaven."

He held the door open for me. The smell was even better inside. Customers filled the register area, and most of the tables were already occupied.

A dark-haired woman sat at the back, her face drawn with grief. I squeezed Hardy's arm. "There."

We walked over and greeted her.

"Hi." She gave us a wan smile. "I'm assuming we're meeting because you found something."

At my look of surprise, she chuckled. "It's like the doctor's office. They always call you and tell you everything is all right. If it's not, they make you set an appointment."

Huh. I never thought of it like that. "May we?"

"Of course. Do you want to get coffee first?"

I did, but I shook my head instead. After this was over, I wasn't sure I'd want it.

Her name was Paige Monroe. She had two grown children and was a grandmother to one. A few streaks of silver at the edge of her temples peeked through her dark hair. She had blue eyes, the first signs of wrinkles showing at their edges. Paige was dressed for work today: dark slacks, a tucked-in printed blouse, a thin brown belt, and matching shoes. She looked put together and stylish, though I wasn't sure she'd still go in today once we finished our meeting.

Hardy declined coffee as well, waving the waitress away when she hovered close by. We might not be in Silverwood Hollow, but small towns were full of nosy people. There were few zip code restrictions when it came to good gossip.

He held a small blue folder with Paige's name and case number on the edge. Before we went to bed last night, we'd painstakingly gone through every picture, discarding most and printing out the ones with the best resolution that showed, without a doubt, Paige's husband engaged in a torrid affair with a younger woman.

Not too much younger, if those pictures were to be believed, but young enough to twist the knife in a little deeper than just the affair would have.

Her shoulders slumped when Hardy set the folder on the table and pushed it over.

"So it's true." It wasn't a question. Tears swam in her eyes, and her lips tightened, thin parentheses lines forming at the edges of her mouth.

"I'm sorry, Mrs. Monroe," Hardy said, his voice steady and even. I glanced at him, suddenly more empathetic than I'd ever been before. How many times had he broken terrible news to people's loved ones? How often had he sat across from someone in their home breaking their hearts?

Under the table, I laid my hand across Hardy's knee. He pressed a warm hand over mine and gave it a gentle squeeze, somehow knowing what I was thinking.

Paige opened the file and drew a shuddering breath, a

tear splashing onto the folder as she flipped through the photos. "I don't know her," she murmured, her eyes fluttering shut. "This isn't the only one," she said, her voice cracking. Paige rubbed a hand over her face. A crack of disbelieving laughter burst from her. "How in the world does an old man have that much time and inclination to engage in multiple affairs?"

It was a question neither of us had the answer to.

She shook her head. "You know, he was never much to look at."

I had to press my lips together to keep from laughing.

Paige saw me and snorted, holding up a picture of the lecherous Mr. Monroe and waving it. "He always had that pot belly and those broken capillaries on his nose. Too much whiskey." She dropped the photo. "I always told him he drank too much. Begged him to stop, actually, but he always told me he had it under control."

Hardy reached over and took Paige's hand. "Mrs. Monroe. You have many options. Whatever you choose to do, you can always call us if you need assistance."

Paige patted his hand. "You're a former police officer, aren't you? I think I read so on your website."

Hardy nodded.

"Then you probably know a good forensic accountant."

A slow smile spread over Hardy's face. "I sure do, ma'am. I'd be happy to forward you her contact information."

"Good. Thank you. This state is equitable instead of

community property, so it's a good thing we have an iron-clad prenuptial agreement."

Hardy's smile sharpened. "If you'd like us to keep him under surveillance, please give us a call."

"I may do that." She nodded to me and dropped the photo back into the folder before she closed it. Paige tapped her fingers on top before pulling it into her purse. "Thank you both for your help." She rose and smoothed the front of her pants. "It will be difficult to pretend everything is fine while I get my ducks in a row, but this news wasn't unexpected."

Paige rummaged in her purse and pulled out a business card. "If you ever find yourself in need of a lawyer, give me a call."

I took the card and skimmed the front. Paige was a contracts lawyer, but below it there was another company listed: *Stone Realty.* Smiling to myself, I thought her ex-husband was about to have a few nasty surprises coming his way.

She left us at the table with a wave. As soon as she stepped out, I waved the server over. After Hardy and I ordered coffees, we both burst out laughing. "As terrible as that was for her to find out, I can't help but think it's going to be worse for him by the time she's done."

Hardy's eyes crinkled with amusement. "A small, evil part of me wants to continue the surveillance for free just to give her more ammunition in her divorce case."

I snickered. My cell phone beeped with an incoming message.

"Ooh," I said once I skimmed the message. "Mrs. Monroe paid and gave us a bonus."

"You're buying dinner," Hardy quipped.

"I'd love to, but first, we have to stop and see Harper. She has a million questions about our engagement dinner."

Hardy groaned.

"We can still elope," I said hopefully.

"No. We'll stop and see her on the way back home." He sipped his coffee and studied me. "What do you think about moving the date?"

My stomach lurched. "Delay? You want to delay our wedding?" I sat my coffee down with a loud clunk, liquid spilling over the top.

Hardy blinked. "What? No." He shook his head frantically. "No! Absolutely not."

My throat worked. "Then what do you mean?"

He reached over and took both my shaking hands. "I mean, do you want to move it earlier? Say...the night of the engagement dinner?"

I stared at him. "Will everyone you want to be there be able to come?"

Hardy smiled. "There's only one person I need to be there. And that's you."

"You mean I don't have to plan a wedding?" I squeaked.

He laughed. "Not if you don't want to."

I thought about it for a long moment. "The only thing I want is to marry you."

Hardy's eyes softened. "Ditto."

"And the people who love us want to see us get married. Not in a restaurant."

He chuckled. "Fair."

"Let's keep to the plan. Smaller wedding. Bigger party."

"And hire a wedding planner."

"And hire a wedding planner," I agreed.

SIX

We were a week away from the dinner. Nerves had settled into my stomach, leaving me a quivering ball of daily anxiety. I never knew how many tiny details went into planning something as innocuous as an engagement dinner, but Fletcher and Harper were in their element, navigating the details with ease.

Speaking of Harper, she and her new beau were still going strong. Too strong, if I were being honest. I'd done my duty as a friend and an adult and kept my mouth shut about it. Harper seemed swept up in a torrent of emotion, sometimes frantic with energy, and other times somber and lost in thought.

I'd never seen her like this, but every time I thought I should say something, I bit my tongue and kept quiet.

"Dakota! You have to pick between regular potatoes and sweet potatoes!"

"Potato Pah-tah-toe. I don't care. What kind do you want?"

Harper blew out an exasperated breath. "I don't like potatoes!"

"Who doesn't like potatoes?" I muttered. "Pick regular, I guess. Sweet potatoes are for fall. Regular potatoes are for always."

Harper made a check mark on her notepad. "Technically, it is fall, so the sweet potato would be a good choice. But I get not wanting to serve them that close to Thanksgiving. Also, they don't have the Wedge salad anymore and need you to pick a new one."

"Ugh." I let out an obnoxious groan.

Harper laughed. "You're such a drama queen."

"Tell me the choices." I laid a hand over my forehead and sighed.

"Caesar or fall," Harper said, rolling her eyes at my dramatics.

"What's *fall?*"

Harper skimmed her notes. "Romaine, pumpkin seeds, apple, pear, roasted pecans, and a poppyseed dressing."

"That sounds better than the Caesar, but can you see if there's an alternative dressing?"

"You don't like poppyseed?"

"It can show up on a drug test. Hardy has a lot of officers coming to the dinner, so better safe than sorry."

Harper made a note. "I'll ask." She set her pad down. "That's it. Fletcher is off, grabbing the rest of the decorations. She finalized all the rest of the food choices yesterday, but passed these to me when they called her back this afternoon."

Relief filled me. "I can't thank you both enough for doing this."

Harper waved my thanks away. "Are you kidding? I live for party planning."

I mock shuddered. "No, thank you."

"Rest assured. Everything is finished. We only need to set things up the day of."

"How much do I owe you?" I pulled out my cellphone. "I can send you a payment really quickly."

"Nothing for me. Just pay the restaurant. Fletcher will give you a receipt when she gets back."

I put my phone away. "Wonderful."

Harper clipped her pen to her notepad and rose. I stopped her before she walked away. "Harper?"

"Hmm?"

"Are you bringing your new beau to the dinner?"

She smiled. "I am. You're going to love him."

I wasn't so sure about that. "How's his apartment search going?"

Harper's eyes flashed with an emotion I couldn't read. It took her a long moment to respond. "He's still looking." She looked away. "But it's okay. I kind of like having someone around."

"What kind of work does he do?"

"He's an art dealer."

I suddenly thought of that social media guy who films himself running across fields waving red flags as he watches videos of people talking about their relationships. "Art? Cool. Fine art?" I shrugged. "Books are my thing. I'm a little hopeless when it comes to art. Daniel is way better at it than I am."

"He's actually opening up a gallery down the road."

My eyebrows lifted. "Wow! How cool. We'll be neighbors. Which building will he be in?"

"I'm not sure. He's dealing with the realtor and still looking at a few properties."

"When he decides on something, let me know, and we'll do a little celebratory dinner welcoming him to town."

Her face lit up. "That sounds wonderful!"

"Good!" I stood and gave her a hug. "I'll call and settle up with the restaurant later. Give me a shout if you need anything from me. Fletcher and I are meeting later."

"Stay away from the martinis!" She gave me a little squeeze and stepped away.

"One time!" I groaned. "Will I never hear the end of that?"

Harper laughed. "It led Hardy back to you, so no. You'll never hear the end of it."

My heart warmed. It *had* led us back together. I'd never take an espresso martini for granted ever again.

Hardy stepped into the shop just as I shrugged my jacket on. "Sorry! I got caught up in chatting. What do you need?"

"All settled. Harper asked about salads and potatoes. Sweet or regular."

Hardy blinked. "Sweet potatoes are a fall vegetable."

I stood on my tiptoes and kissed him on the jaw. "I said the exact same thing. Ready to go?"

"Sure." He held my purse while I tugged on my gloves, then held the door open.

I waited until we were in the car and a few miles away from the shop before I spoke.

"I think Harper is getting love-bombed," I blurted.

Hardy took his attention off the road for a brief second, glancing at me in surprise. "What?"

"This guy she's seeing."

"Ah." I'd vented about him a few times to Hardy. He listened and advised me to stay out of it, which I'd done, but this was going too far. "Why do you think that?"

"He's still living with her."

Hardy stayed silent.

"I don't think he's even looking for a place!"

He reached over and laid a hand on my knee. "Dakota."

I sighed. "Don't say it. I know."

He turned down our street. "Sometimes we have to let the people we care about make the mistakes we can see coming a mile away."

"But what if he hurts her?"

He lifted a shoulder. "Again, sometimes it's the only way to learn."

"I mean physically."

He gave me a sharp look. "Has he said or done anything to make you think that way?"

"No," I grumbled. "I have a bad feeling I can't shake, though."

"Then we'll keep an eye on him."

My shoulders slumped.

"Intuition is a powerful thing, Dakota. I've learned never to discount it. If you think something bad is on the horizon, we'll pay attention."

"Thank you."

"No need to thank me. My intuition has saved me more times than I can count."

We drove in silence the rest of the way, my thoughts swirling over Harper and this mysterious beau of hers.

SEVEN

The unspoken rule of wearing white to a wedding never sat right with me. A bride should be able to wear whatever she wanted.

I decided on blush pink—still a bridal color, but not white.

The skirt was made of soft tulle, which swirled and swished when I moved. I'd chosen a cool gray, off-the-shoulder cashmere top and matching kitten heels. Mom had given me a pearl-drop necklace that Gran passed to her when she married. It matched my top but had a slight iridescent sheen to it.

I'd paired it with small diamond drops that glimmered in the light when I moved my head—a gift from Hardy after he proposed.

My hands trembled as I fastened the dainty silver toggle bracelet. I had nothing to be nervous about, but it didn't stop the anxiety roaring through my blood.

The door opened. Hardy poked his head in, his eyes widening as he spotted me.

He wore a dove gray suit with a blush pocket square. "Wow," he croaked.

My cheeks heated. "Wow yourself." I turned and adjusted the square, smoothing my hands over his chest. "How's Izzy?"

"Your mom is still fussing over her hair."

We grinned at each other. Izzy had asked for curls. Big ones. Not the kind you did with the straightener. I wouldn't have known the difference until Mom pulled up a video. Who knew she used social media more than I did?

She arrived this morning armed with a massive bag of makeup, hair products, and curling irons. When Izzy saw her, she'd squealed with delight and launched herself into Mom's arms.

The sight of it made me melt, but Mom's lips quivered as she picked Izzy up and held her tight. Our eyes had met, and Mom's looked grateful and hopeful.

It had both healed and broken my heart all over again. We'd never be Izzy's blood family, but the wonderful thing about family was you could choose it, and sometimes it could choose you.

Gran had pulled up sometime afterward, and the three had sequestered themselves in the guest bathroom for hours.

"How much time do we have left before we need to leave?"

Hardy glanced at the silver watch he wore. "Half an hour."

"I'll go check on the Three Musketeers."

He grinned and held the door open for me. "Don't let Izzy hog them if you need them."

"I can share. Mom and Gran would throw themselves on the ground and let Izzy use them as a walking path. I'm under no delusion of my new number in the pecking order."

"That's what I'm afraid of," Hardy murmured. "Izzy is way too cute for her own good."

I laughed. "She is, but Mom and Gran have been around the block. They know the wiles of the female child."

The sound of delighted giggles came from behind the door seconds after I knocked.

Gran answered, a cloud of hairspray coming from behind her. She gasped when she saw me. "Dakota! You look gorgeous!"

Gran held open the door so I could walk in. Izzy sat on a small stool, her dark hair perfectly curled into identical ringlets all over her head. She wore a blush dress with a princess skirt, the same color as mine, and gray slippers with white tights.

"You look adorable! And your hair looks so good!" I cooed.

She blinked wide blue eyes up at me. "Thank you. Gigi made every curl perfect."

"She sure did," I agreed, picking up one of her ringlets.

I met Mom's eyes in the mirror. "Almost ready to go?"

Everyone was dressed and had their hair and makeup done. Mom and Gran wore blush dresses, both in different styles. Mom preferred a more form-fitting dress, and Gran preferred loose, whimsical, and sparkly, so her dress was a little more similar to mine than Mom's.

Mom wore a blush sheath dress with gray heels and had done her hair into loose curls. Gran wore a tulle skirt, but it was gray, and a blush pink wrap sweater. Her hair floated around her head in a riot of silver curls.

Pride swelled inside of me. Three generations of Adair women. A future fourth, made not by name but by love, kicked her feet to and fro, watching Mom in the mirror as she pinned one last curl. Tears swam in my eyes, and I blinked them away so I wouldn't mess my mascara up.

Gran clicked her tongue. "Aww, honey." She cupped my chin and smiled, warmth in her blue eyes. "Don't cry. There's plenty of time for tears later."

Mom sniffed. "If you cry, I'll cry, and it will be a real mess in here."

Izzy patted Mom's arm. "Don't cry, Gigi."

Mom kissed the top of Izzy's head and cleared her throat. "We can't promise anything," she told her, before she rose and smoothed her hands down the sides of her dress. "All right. I think we're done here. You ready to go face the town and tell them Silverwood Hollow's most eligible bachelor is off the market?"

Gran snickered.

"Mom!"

. . .

THE RESTAURANT WAS NEW, but already had a reputation for excellent food and even better ambiance. Fletcher and Harper insisted I do absolutely nothing except show up the day of the dinner, and as hard as it was, I obliged.

Both women stood outside waiting for me. They waved happily when they saw me, and hurried over to the car. Fletcher let out a gasp when she saw Izzy, lifting her into her arms and swinging her around, making Izzy giggle.

"You look like a proper little princess!" Fletcher exclaimed. She set Izzy down and curtsied. "Pray tell, Princess Izzy, how may we serve you today?"

Izzy wrinkled her nose as she thought about it. "Cake?" she asked.

Everyone laughed. I slid out of the car. "After dinner."

She sighed in disappointment.

Fletcher bent down. "We have three kinds of cake," she whispered. "If you're really good, maybe Miss Dakota will let you try one of each."

Izzy's eyes lit up at the possibility. With an impish grin, she skipped up the stairs to wait for us by the door.

"She's adorable," Harper said, eyes sparkling as she watched Izzy.

"And you," Fletcher added, "look like a real-life Disney princess." She made a circle motion with her index finger. Obliging her, I did a little turn. "That skirt is to die for."

Mom got out next, and Hardy came around to the

passenger side just in time to help Gran. She tsked at him but smiled as she took his hand and stepped out of the vehicle.

"And you, Hardy," Fletcher murmured, wiggling her eyebrows as her gaze slid from him to me, "look delectable."

Mom snorted. "Fletcher. You got a pretty delectable one at your heels. Leave Dakota's alone."

Fletcher grinned at Mom. "You always take the fun out of stuff."

I shook my head at their antics. Mom and Fletcher got along like a house on fire—so well, in fact, they sometimes hung out without me. At first, I thought it was weird, but then I remembered how awesome Mom was and how anyone would be lucky to have her in their lives.

Mom rolled her eyes and slung an arm over Fletcher's shoulders. "Thank you for doing this for my daughter."

Fletcher put her arm around Mom's waist, and they walked upstairs together.

Hardy escorted Gran up the steps, smiling as he walked past us. Butterflies flipped in my stomach. Once I finally got past my fear of the unknown, I never wavered in my decision concerning him or Izzy. I'd never waver when it came to them ever again.

Harper shut the passenger door. "You ready?"

I squared my shoulders. "I'd much rather have pizza at home, but yes."

She chuckled. "I always say funerals are for the living,

but weddings and all their events kind of feel the same way, don't they? Especially for us introverts."

"Exactly," I breathed. "It feels like I'm a doll on one of those slowly spinning pedestals, and everyone is staring at me."

Hardy held the door open while everyone filed in, holding me back by the elbow once everyone was through.

I stared up at him.

"You ready?"

"Harper asked me the same thing."

He grinned. "Everyone wants to see you."

I put my hand against his chest. "I doubt that. Everyone is here to see you, former detective."

His expression sobered. "You have no idea how many people you've helped." Hardy shook his head. "You're an integral part of this town. One day, I hope you'll realize it." He rested his hand on the small of my back. "Now, let's go have a party."

EIGHT

Everyone in town must have shown up this evening. I walked around the room marveling at all the faces—those I recognized and some I didn't. Hardy kept a light grip on my elbow as we moved through the dining area, greeting every one of the smiling faces. Twenty minutes in, and I thought I was going to collapse from social fatigue.

All the *hellos* and *congratulations* and *oh my goodness, I'm so happy for yous* had taken their toll on my psyche. It was wonderful and exciting, but also exhausting. My cheeks felt stiff and my smile frozen in place as I shook hands and murmured polite *thank yous*.

I did a lot around town, and it required me to talk to many people, but I'd yet to form very many friendships. Hardy dealt with people daily, digging into their relationships and unveiling their deepest secrets, but everyone still flocked around him like moths to a flame.

I envied people who could form relationships so easily.

It always took more for me. Small talk felt like dying a slow death, so having Hardy with me to chat with everyone around us put me a little more at ease.

Izzy charmed the room with her happy smile. She showed her pretty dress and sparkly shoes to everyone she talked to. Eventually, Mom came over and eased me away from Hardy, smiling apologetically at the crowd still gathered around us.

"Apologies. I need to borrow my daughter for a few minutes for some last-minute decisions before the dinner starts." Mom wrapped her arm around my shoulders and steered me through the room, all the way into the back, close to the kitchen. She stopped me and took both my hands.

"Breathe," she said quietly.

I blinked at her.

"Dakota." Mom placed both her hands on either side of my face. "Take a breath."

I closed my eyes and inhaled.

"Good. Again."

I dragged in another deep breath, then another until my heart stopped beating like a drum.

When I opened my eyes, Mom still stood there. "I'd forgotten how you get in a crowd when you're the object of attention." She smiled sadly. "Do you need a Xanax?"

I laughed. "Mom!"

She chuckled. "You may laugh, but I'm serious." Mom dug around in her purse and pulled out a bottle. She shook it, the small pills rattling around. "I keep them in my purse because you never know when a panic attack is right around the corner."

"I'm okay. Thank you for getting me out of there." I shook my head and waved the pills away. "This is a night I need to remember."

Mom reached over and drew me into a hug. "You ready to go back out?"

I exhaled. "Yes. Sorry about that."

Harper came around the corner wearing an odd look. She didn't see us until she was almost upon us. "Oh! Dakota."

"Everything okay?" Mom asked.

Harper forced a smile. "Yes. Of course!"

"Are you sure?" I asked, not believing her for an instant.

"All good," Harper assured us. "What are you doing in here?"

The door opened. A dark head peeked inside, eyes sweeping until they fell on me. Relief filled Hardy's gaze. "There you are." He glanced at Mom and Harper, his brow furrowing. "Is this a conference I didn't know about?"

I walked over to him and brushed my lips over his. "I was on my way out."

"Good. People are asking about you. If you need another moment, I'll cover for you."

I slid an arm around his waist and let him lead me out. Mom and Harper stayed behind. I spared a moment to wonder if I should press Harper a little harder. Something was definitely wrong, but I saw nothing amiss.

Hardy led me straight to the table, holding my chair out for me as I settled in. He poured us both a glass of wine and settled beside me.

"You hate this, don't you?"

I glanced at him in surprise. "I—"

"It's okay to admit it. Parties have never been my thing."

I smiled sheepishly. "Do you hate this?"

Hardy shrugged. "I'm used to them, I guess. Police officers have to do a lot of events, and we're constantly talking to people. Wouldn't say I love them, though." He squeezed my knee. "Things will calm down, especially once they start serving dinner."

"I'm starving," I admitted.

Fletcher sank into the chair beside me and blew out a breath. "This place is very people-y today!"

I laughed. "Sure is. You're used to it, I presume?"

She shrugged. "I suppose. Not so much anymore. I used to work in a lot of crowds, but ever since coming to a small town, I do more one-on-ones than anything." Fletcher looked around. "Where's Harper?"

I jerked a thumb over my shoulder. "In the back with Mom."

Fletcher frowned. "Have you talked to her?"

"Briefly. She seemed a little out of sorts."

"She's been like that for a couple of days now." Fletcher shook her head. "I couldn't get her to say what's wrong."

I wondered if it had anything to do with that boyfriend of hers. "Did she bring her new beau?"

"Mmm," Fletcher said, the noise full of disapproval.

Hardy's brows inched up. "You don't care for him?"

Fletcher snagged the wine bottle and poured herself a glass. "I've met a lot of people over the years in the job I'm in. You learn to read people quickly." She took a sip of wine. "That guy of hers." She slowly shook her head. "He's no good, Dakota. But neither you nor I can tell her. She's going to have to figure it out for herself."

I nodded. "Where is he?"

Fletcher looked around the room. "I haven't seen him in a while. The last time I checked, he was in the kitchen arguing with Harper."

"About what?" Hardy asked. He had an odd look on his face.

"Couldn't tell you." Her lips tightened. "But Harper looked frightened." She set her glass down. "Maybe I should go find her."

"Mom's with her," I assured her.

Fletcher sighed. "Good."

THE DOORS to the kitchen opened. Several servers came out holding large trays.

"Ah," Fletcher declared. "Dinner is served!"

My stomach growled as soon as she finished the sentence, making us all laugh.

. . .

WE ATE TOO much and drank a little too much, but once people had settled in at their tables, the dinner became a lot more enjoyable. Hardy pulled my chair closer, draping an arm over the back of my chair. I leaned my head on his shoulder and watched as Mom, Gran, and Izzy tore up the dance floor.

Harper bustled around all the tables, stopping to talk with almost everyone, but there was a tension in her frame I'd never seen before. She was always so easygoing that this new mood had me worried. I murmured to Hardy that I was going to check on her and rose from my seat, winding through the tables until I stopped in front of her.

She smiled, but it failed to reach her eyes. "Enjoying yourself?"

I took both of her hands. She blinked in surprise, her lips curving into a real smile this time.

"I want you to take the next few days off. There's no way I can thank you for what you've done for me. At a minimum, I can give you a few freebie days off and treat you and your new guy to dinner soon."

Her eyes flashed. "Ah. Well. I'm not so sure he's my guy anymore."

"Oh?" I felt like I'd been prying too much when I asked her about him, so this time, I waited for her to tell me.

She dropped her eyes and tugged my hand, pulling me away from the crowd and into a darker corner close to the restrooms. "He's seeing someone else."

"Oh, Harper." I reached in for a hug. "I'm so sorry."

She dashed a tear away. "Someone sent me an e-mail with pictures." A watery laugh escaped her. "It's not only one girl."

"Is he still here?"

"I haven't seen him for a while. He must have left. There was no reason for him to stay."

I'd say. "You want to come over tonight? We can have a slumber party."

Harper shook her head. "No. That's okay. I should have waited to confront him. I'm so sorry for messing up your party."

I shook my head. "No. Never. Are you kidding? This party is amazing! Everything is wonderful, and the food is to die for."

Fletcher found us and put her arms around our shoulders. "Uh oh. Serious girl talk going down over here. What's up?"

I told Fletcher. She grimaced. "Oh, honey. I'm so sorry."

Harper sniffed. "I know you didn't like him."

I winced.

Fletcher shrugged. "You're right. He isn't good enough for you. I make no apologies."

"Regardless, this guy is out of your life now." A thought occurred to me. "When is he moving out?"

Fletcher sucked in a breath. "He's *living* with you?"

Harper groaned and sank against the wall. "I'm so dumb!" She slapped a hand to her face.

"No," I disagreed. "You're human. I can only assume he's done this quite a bit."

Fletcher nodded. "There's a name for guys like that. Maybe Dakota can ask Hardy to come over to your house and help him get his stuff out."

"I'm sure he'd be happy to." It wasn't ideal on the night of our engagement party, but if it got the guy out of her house faster, I'm sure he'd agree.

"Not tonight," Harper said. "I'm going to stay at a hotel and head home tomorrow. Maybe he can help me then?"

"I'll ask." I reached out and gave her another hug. "I better get back, but you let me know if you need anything."

She gave me a squeeze and stepped away.

"Thank you both for all the work you put into this," I said, as I stepped out of the hallway and back into the main area.

"Stop thanking us!" they called back at the same time.

Grinning, I headed back to my table. Hardy still sat there watching Izzy do the hokey pokey.

"Everything okay?" he asked.

"It will be."

He glanced down at me.

"She broke up with that guy."

Relief flashed in his eyes. "Does this guy have a name?"

"I never asked," I admitted sheepishly.

Hardy chuckled. "Never expected him to last, I take it?"

"I hoped not."

"What happened?"

"He's cheating with multiple girls."

Hardy winced. "Poor Harper."

"She's staying at a hotel tonight and will head home tomorrow."

"Want me to head over with her to ensure he gets everything out?"

I grinned. "Already volunteered you."

A COUPLE OF HOURS LATER, only a few people milled around in the restaurant. We'd said our goodbyes to everyone and just needed to settle the bill.

I'd just signed it when a bloodcurdling scream rang out.

Hardy spun, his hand on his hip, searching for the weapon he rarely carried these days. With a muffled curse, he sprinted toward the back. I snatched my card and shoved it into my purse and followed.

Fletcher stayed close on my heels as we skidded around the corner. Hardy stood off to the side, his face a blank mask. Harper was on her knees, her hands covered in blood. She hovered over a prone body with a rapidly growing bloodstain underneath it.

Male. Leanly built with a visible tattoo peeking from underneath the sleeve on his left arm. This had to be Harper's...whatever he was to her.

"Call 911," Hardy urged.

Fletcher scrambled for her phone.

"Harper," Hardy said, moving to crouch down beside her. "I need you to step away."

"No, no, no," she whispered. "What happened? What did—"

"Stop talking," Hardy said in a grating voice. "Wait for the police."

He helped her up, careful not to step in the blood, and gently steered her over to the far wall. Our eyes locked, and I could tell Hardy was extremely concerned. I came over and stood beside Harper's trembling form.

"Police are on the way," Fletcher said, her gaze bouncing back and forth between us before lingering on the body lying on the floor.

"I thought Aaron left." Harper's voice shook. "We had a f-f-fight, and he left me in the kitchen and—"

"Harper," Hardy warned, his gaze sweeping over the room. "I think you should call a lawyer."

My attention snapped to him. Hardy's expression was grim. "Is that really necessary?" I asked.

"It's my professional opinion," he said, which told me a lot. Hardy was wondering if Harper had done this.

I looked away and squeezed my eyes shut briefly as I tried to calm my racing thoughts. First, there was no way she'd done this.

Second, if Hardy told Harper to get a lawyer, it looked like she *had* done this.

Third...there was no third. Harper was in deep trouble.

"Dakota?" her voice wobbled.

I stepped closer, careful to avoid the blood on her clothing. "I'm here."

"I'm scared."

Fletcher came over to stand beside us. "We're here. We won't go anywhere until we have to."

Harper's head dropped. Tears spilled down her face. "I swear I didn't do this."

"We know," I said.

"Hardy thinks I did."

I exhaled. "Hardy was a detective for a long time. If he told you to get a lawyer, I'd listen to him." Confirming her fears would help no one.

Fletcher punched something into her cellphone and stepped away, speaking quietly to whoever was on the other line. We stood in grim silence for several minutes until she came back over.

"I've called a lawyer for you."

Harper's head snapped up. "You didn't have to."

Fletcher held a hand up. "I know I didn't. You need one, and I'm able to help."

Harper sagged in relief. "Thank you," she whispered.

"It's nothing," Fletcher insisted. "He'll be here in twenty minutes. Say nothing to the police until he gets here."

I didn't like this. It was necessary, but it still felt squirmy to me. I'd been involved in more cases than I could count and had never once felt the need to employ a lawyer. And Hardy had never once suggested one.

A bad feeling settled into my bones.

Maybe if we'd eloped, none of this would have happened.

NINE

We dragged ourselves home a few hours later, Izzy passed out against Hardy's chest as we went inside. I kicked off my shoes and collapsed on the couch while he tucked Izzy in. When he walked inside the living room tugging his tie loose, I waved wearily at him.

Hardy kicked off his shoes and sat on the couch, lifting my feet to put on his lap. I arched my foot when he pressed his thumb into a sore spot.

"I never thought our engagement party would end in murder, but I've found anything is possible when you're around." He didn't sound angry, more bemused than anything.

I groaned. "Izzy doesn't know anything, does she?"

Hardy shook his head. "Your mom and Gran kept her shielded from everything, and one of the officers took her out to the car to show her how all the buttons worked while the rest investigated."

"That was nice of him."

"He has three daughters at home."

I winced. "Bet that house has lots of emotions."

Hardy chuckled. "He loves every minute of it."

We were carefully avoiding the conversation I knew we needed to have. There was no way I'd let Harper take the fall for a murder I knew she didn't commit.

"Hardy?"

His fingers stilled. The silence between us drew out. "Of course we'll take the case."

My shoulders slumped in relief. He always knew exactly what I needed before I gave voice to it. "Do you think she's guilty?"

"I think it looks bad. Really bad. But do I think she's a murderer" He shook his head. "I've met far too many murderers in my day, and Harper has nothing in common with any of them."

I let out a sigh of relief.

"But Dakota?"

"Hmm?" I loved Hardy's foot rubs, and he was never stingy with them.

"Harper might not be a murderer, but it doesn't mean she didn't kill him."

I blinked and sat up a little straighter. "What does that mean?"

"We don't know what happened yet. Harper could still be involved."

"She said she didn't do it!"

Hardy raised a placating hand. "I know what she said,

but I also know what the evidence looks like. She just found out he was cheating on her and that he was a con man. It would make a saint angry."

I refused to believe it.

"I'm not saying she murdered him," he said in a gentle voice. "But maybe something happened. Maybe she pushed him, and he fell. Maybe it was some other kind of accident. I don't know. We will have to wait and see what the coroner says."

I didn't get close enough to the body to see what happened. All I'd seen was the pool of blood. "Do you know what happened?"

"It looks like he was shot at least once."

"Shot?" I blurted. "How in the world did we not hear anything?"

"Silencer," Hardy said. "Plus, we had a DJ. It's possible a gun could have gone off during an upbeat song and we wouldn't have heard a thing."

"Harper doesn't have a gun. There's no way she shot him."

"Getting a copy of the autopsy may take a while, but this state considers them public record. If I can get the info sooner, it will help us piece together what happened."

"Do you know Harper's lawyer?" I noticed him on the way out, once the police had finished questioning us. He was a tall, handsome man wearing a dark suit and a grim expression.

"No. Though I don't often deal with lawyers unless I have to. I've never seen him before."

"Maybe he can help us."

"Everything would have to go through Harper. She's his client and has to authorize everything."

I allowed my head to drop back onto the pillow. "Something tells me she won't mind."

"Her bail hearing is soon. I think they'll allow it. Once she's out, we will need to work quickly. Whoever this was is still on the loose." He patted my calf and slid my legs out of the way. "Now come on. Let's go to bed."

To my surprise, he scooped me up and carried me into the bedroom, shutting the door behind us with a well-placed kick.

I looped my arms around his neck. "Whatever you say."

Hardy grinned and pressed a kiss to my lips. "Good. It's been a long day, future Mrs. Cavanaugh."

The words sent a shiver of anticipation down my spine.

IT TOOK a full 48 hours for Harper to make bail. The first thing she did when she got out was call me. I'd just shut the bookstore down for the day when my phone rang.

"Harper!" I breathed in relief.

"Hi, Dakota. I'm so sorry I missed my shift."

I snorted. "Are you kidding? How many shifts did I miss when I was running around playing detective?"

Her laugh sounded tired. "True, but now you really are playing detective, aren't you? Speaking of, do you think you and Fletcher can meet me at my house in an hour?"

"I'll text Fletcher, but I'm happy to come. Should I bring anything?"

"Wine?" Harper asked hopefully.

"You got it. I'll grab some takeout, too. Craving anything?"

"I could go for a big fat slice of pepperoni pizza."

"I'll pick up a couple of pizzas on my way. Be careful going home."

"See you soon."

We disconnected, and I texted Fletcher. She responded almost right away and said she'd bring mixers—whatever that meant—and ended with a wink emoji.

This will not end like martini night!

She responded with: *Or will it?*

Sighing, I called out for Poppy, who came running over. I scooped her up and grabbed the rest of my stuff. Harper would love seeing the cat, and Poppy always loved exploring Harper's backyard area. Lots of places to hide and pounce on unsuspecting lizards.

FLETCHER and I made it at the same time. She held a canvas bag that clinked suspiciously and gave me a mysterious smile when I gave her the hairy eyeball.

Fletcher knocked on the door. Harper answered, and I choked down a gasp of dismay.

She looked like she'd aged ten years since yesterday.

Her posture was drooped, and dark shadows clung to the undersides of her eyes. She'd tossed her hair into a high messy bun and her face was devoid of makeup. Harper was always stunning even without makeup, but today, she looked like she'd given up.

She wore a pair of blue joggers and a white tank top with a long cardigan. Her feet were bare. Harper tried to smile when she waved us in, but it fell a moment later.

I stepped in and headed straight to the kitchen because my arms were full. "I have to run back out to the car to grab something else, so give me just a second."

Harper didn't acknowledge me, but she did head straight for the pizza, so that was a hopeful sign. Fletcher gave me a meaningful look as I hurried out.

Poppy pressed her face to the window and yowled pitifully.

I scoffed. "You've been in there for less than a minute and you're acting like I left you in there on purpose."

Poppy stared at me.

"Like I've ever forgotten about you."

She pawed the window. With a laugh, I opened the door and scooped her up, dropping a kiss on top of her fuzzy head. "Be nice to Miss Harper. She's having a really hard time right now."

Poppy huffed like I'd offended her.

Harper squealed when she saw whom I held, her face showing more animation than it had in a while. I held Poppy out to her. She scooped the cat up, pressed her face into her fur, and kissed her multiple times before she hurried into the living room and plopped onto the couch, still chatting away.

Fletcher stared at them. "I brought top-shelf vodka, and the cat gets more attention?"

I laughed. "It's hard to resist the allure of a fuzzy cat when your world is falling apart."

"Huh," she said, and set the bottle down. "Maybe I should look into getting one of those fuzzballs."

I stared at her. "Maybe spend some time with Poppy first. Some people aren't cat people."

"I like a cat's independence," Fletcher said, handing me a plate. "But I also like how sweet Poppy is being to her."

Indeed. Harper had resorted from baby talk to full-on sobbing into Poppy's fur, and my stalwart cat just sat there purring.

I grimaced and grabbed another plate for Harper, filling both with slices. I took one over to her and went back for the wine. Fletcher had made herself a vodka tonic. She waved the bottle at me and raised her eyebrows in a question.

"Not a chance," I said.

Fletcher poked her bottom lip out in a pout.

"I'll take one," Harper said, her words muffled by Poppy's fur.

Fletcher took a bigger glass out of Harper's cabinet and made her a double. I wasn't so sure that was the best idea, but sometimes a stiff drink and a fluffy cat made the world a little brighter, so I wouldn't begrudge her.

Fletcher and I settled ourselves in Harper's small living room and waited for Harper to compose herself. I wasn't sure why she'd invited either of us, though the obvious reason was to discuss what happened and make a game plan.

Poppy continued being the perfect kitty and let Harper snuggle her. Those two worked in the shop alone quite a bit, but I had no idea they'd bonded that much. The thought warmed me. Poppy took a while to make friends, but when she did, she was as loyal and friendly as could be. Even so, there was something almost supernatural about her and her ability to gauge someone's mood and act in an appropriate manner.

Take Harper, for example. The woman was using Poppy as a kitty pillow right now, and Poppy was boneless and purring.

Fletcher sipped her vodkatini and watched them with a bemused expression.

It took a few minutes, but Harper finally uncurled herself from my cat, sat up, and took the pizza with a word of thanks. Poppy adjusted herself until she was firmly in Harper's lap, then curled into a ball and went right to sleep.

"Thanks for coming," she said, after she'd taken a couple of bites.

"Any time." I sipped my wine and studied her. She had a little more color in her face now, and her hands didn't tremble as she held her plate.

"And thank you for the lawyer referral, Fletcher. He's wonderful."

Fletcher grinned. "I should hope so. He's my brother."

My eyes widened. "What?"

She shrugged. "He's thinking about moving here and was visiting for a few days."

I snorted. "I'm sure he was ecstatic about you calling him in the middle of the night to come out for a case."

She laughed and waved a hand. "He's a textbook workaholic and happy to do it. In fact, it gave him the opportunity to see what kind of place Silverwood is."

"I'm sure he didn't expect a murder," Harper murmured.

"Nothing surprises him," Fletcher said. "He's the most unflappable person I know."

"What's his name?" I asked.

"Sean O'Day. I don't know how he skipped the ginger curse, but he's got himself a head full of ebony hair and devilish green eyes, and I have to put on sunscreen if I even think about looking out a window!" She shook her head but wore a fond smile, and I could see the love she had for him.

"There are a few spaces downtown he can lease if he decides to stay. If he needs a temporary space to work while he looks, I'm happy to share a portion of the P.I. office."

"That's so generous! I'll let him know. It might work out well since he's representing Harper, and she'll be right there if he needs anything from her." Fletcher reached over for the wine bottle and poured more into Harper's glass. "Now, tell us how we can help."

Harper drew in a shuddering breath. "It looks really bad for me." Her eyes were drawn and haunted. She looked away from us, at a spot on the far wall as she spoke. "I had motive and opportunity, and he was living with me."

Fletcher and I locked gazes. While this was true, I knew Harper didn't have a mean bone in her body. Fletcher hadn't known her nearly as long as I had, and from the look on her face, I knew she'd agree with me.

"That doesn't mean anything," I insisted.

Harper's nostrils flared. "It means everything!" She closed her eyes and took a deep breath. "I'm sorry. I didn't mean to snap. It's just—"

"No," I insisted. "You don't have to apologize. I'm the one who's sorry. Minimizing the seriousness isn't helping anything. But I know you didn't do this. That's why I'm so confident we'll find out who did."

She exhaled and sagged against the couch cushions. "Thank you. I'm glad someone believes in me."

Fletcher pulled a small notebook and pen from her purse. "Dakota is right. But to help you, we need to know everything."

Everything, as it turned out, blew my mind.

TEN

Sean O'Day was a handsome devil. Tall, dark-haired, and dark-eyed, I knew the women of this town would be beating his door down if he decided to move here. He knocked on the door of the P.I. firm early the next morning. Hardy answered the door to let him in. Even at the early hour, the lawyer was dressed in a suit, his shoes perfectly shined, and his jacket pressed.

He stuck his hand out to greet Hardy and nodded to me when Hardy introduced me. I was busy trying to get the safe open to stick the notes we'd taken on Harper's case inside. When I saw who it was, I stood and walked over to the desk. He may need some of the information if he was here to talk about her.

"Morning, Mr. O'Day," I said.

"Morning. Please call me Sean." He gave me a harried smile. "My sister mentioned something about potentially renting a desk here to give me some time to look around town?"

Hardy glanced at me. Oops. I'd forgotten to mention it to him.

"Yes. I saw her last night at Harper's." I gestured to the smaller desk toward the back of the room. "We aren't using it right now, so you're welcome to it. There's no need for payment. I'm happy to help Fletcher out."

His eyes brightened. "Well, that's wonderful. I promise to be quiet and respectful. Harper's case is the only one I have right now, though I'll have to consult with a local attorney due to my out-of-state license. If you have a good recommendation, please let me know. Contrary to popular belief, we don't all know each other." A rueful grin slid over his face.

"I'll ask around," I said.

"Would you like a cup of coffee or tea?" Hardy asked.

"Coffee would be great. Thanks."

I showed him to the empty desk. "Harper is obviously taking a few days off, but she works right in there." I pointed to the doors. "I own the bookstore on the other side."

"Bookstore?" Curiosity lit his face. "Do you carry all genres?"

A fellow booklover? Sean might be as likable as his sister. "Absolutely. I carry several local authors but also have all the current bestsellers."

"Can I go through those doors any time?"

"Only when it's open. I keep the same hours as the bookstore and lock those doors when I close up."

"Good to know. I brought an e-reader with me, but I prefer turning actual pages."

"Me too." I smiled at him and stepped away from the desk. "I'll let you settle in here. Hardy and I will be in and out today. Please make yourself at home."

Hardy walked back in with a cup of coffee and set it in front of Sean, along with a small pile of napkins, a coffee stirrer, and cream and sugar. "There's more in the shop area if you want it. Dakota has a small bar set up with everything you need."

"Thank you." He shook his head. "I can't believe how welcoming everyone is here."

"Welcome to Silverwood Hollow." My smile sharpened. "Now please get my friend out of her murder charges and you'll be like family."

Sean blinked, surprise flashing over his face until he realized I was joking.

Mostly.

"I will do my best," he said quietly, before picking up the coffee and taking a sip.

"That's all we ask." I looped my arm into Hardy's and grabbed my stuff, including the notes I'd kept out of the safe. Sean hadn't asked about them, and they might help me today, so I'd take them with me and put them away later.

"Ready?"

Hardy nodded and grabbed his jacket. "We'll be back in a little while."

Sean already had his head buried in a legal text. He gave us a distracted wave as we headed out.

"Where to first?" Hardy asked when we were settled in the car with the heat cranked up.

"Brown sugar latte?" I asked hopefully.

Hardy groaned good-naturedly. "You're going to turn into a latte if you don't cool it on the coffee consumption."

I poked him in the ribs good naturedly. "Just like you and your good whiskey consumption?" He collected Irish and Scottish whiskies, something I never knew about him until I moved in. Hardy never indulged too much, but every once in a while, usually after a particularly stressful day, I'd find him in the study nursing a small glass of the amber liquid, contemplating life in his leather recliner.

Hardy laughed. "I'll take my chances. A couple times a week is much better than daily lattes."

I sighed. "You're right. Last one this week. I swear. I'll keep it to regular coffee for a while."

"Promise?"

I winced. "Maybe?"

He snorted. "I don't care about your latte consumption, but those things are high in sugar and other things we can't pronounce."

"I know you're right, but the heart wants what the heart wants."

Hardy put his signal on and turned into the coffee

shop parking lot. "And right now the heart wants a brown sugar latte?"

"It really does."

Hardy chuckled and pulled into the drive-through.

NURSING the small latte a few minutes later and careful not to spill it on my notes, Hardy asked me to read off the list of potential suspects again.

He knew a few of them, a fact that hadn't surprised me. Hardy knew just about everyone in this town and the bordering towns, and rattled off facts about them I hastily jotted down.

He had me cross through a couple of them immediately. A man named Jenkins, who Hardy had said was 85 years old and had just broken his hip; a woman named Collette, who had just given birth to twins; and a college student named Rebecca, who'd dropped out two semesters ago.

"You don't have to scratch them completely, but they're the least likely or capable of committing this crime. Now. Who do we have left?"

I rattled off the names. Fifteen to be exact.

"Still too many," Hardy growled.

"Any name we can scratch off right away is excellent work. I don't know anyone on this list, so I was zero help." I frowned at the list in my hand. "I think I'm going to talk to Cole about this."

Hardy grunted in acknowledgement. "I think that's a

good idea. He's been around for a long time and might have dealt with them in his work capacity. I wouldn't put anything in e-mail, though."

I snorted. Our last case had scarred us both. Daniel Jenkins has been the victim of a cyber stalker who'd planted cameras the size of a nailhead in his house. He'd also had his computer hacked and his manuscript stolen, sending Hardy and me into a paranoid spiral of desperation as we tried to ensure that would never happen to us. We had new virus software, swept both shops for listening devices, cameras, and spyware, and added extra security into our own surveillance to prevent hackers from overtaking it.

The world had gotten way too advanced, and I'd gotten way too complacent to realize it. Even Hardy had seemed taken aback by the technology we'd pulled out of Daniel's house, and if a police officer could be surprised, we had a lot of catching up to do.

So, as was Hardy's way, we'd hired the best to help us, and now our security was on par with Fort Knox. I told Hardy I drew the line at not knowing how the remote controls or the computers worked, so whatever we did had to be simple to operate. I was happy to say even though the new television remote had way more buttons than I felt it needed, I only needed to know how to use three of them. On, off, and volume. The little cursor moved wherever I wanted it to, so I knew how to use it to click, too.

"Let's swing by his office and see if he's in." It would

give me the opportunity to see Fletcher and let her know Sean was settling in nicely, if she didn't already know.

Hardy nodded and took a right at the next light. I settled in for the drive, marveling at the changes my life had gone through over the last several months. First, it was nice having a man to drive me around. I never loved getting behind the wheel, and Hardy never batted an eye when it came to driving. In fact, the few times I'd felt guilty about it and tried to take the keys, he'd given me a weird look and shook his head.

Yes, it was a little macho, but I liked it. There were some traditional things about us, but there were some things so odd in our pairing I still couldn't believe we'd somehow made it work. I'd never be the kind of woman who gave up a job or important work. I had a lot of options now, thanks to the discovery of those Audubon manuscripts some time back. If I wanted to, I could give it all up and never work another day in my life.

But that wasn't my personality. I knew I'd never be happy doing nothing, even if it was exploring the world. I had to feel needed, and I needed to feel like I was making a difference. If not in my own life, then in someone else's. And now, we had Izzy, and I was about to step into her life as a stepmother. The pressure was immense, but I knew I'd try my absolute best to fill the void I knew she felt every single day. It would never be perfect for her, but I hoped she would eventually see how much I loved her, and how badly I wanted her to thrive.

Hardy twined his fingers in mine. "Penny for your thoughts."

I smiled. "We could leave everything behind and retire to a nice little cabin in the woods, if we wanted. Maybe hire Izzy the best tutor money could buy, and we could spend our days fishing for trout in a little stream somewhere on our land and spend our nights by the fire."

Hardy gave me a funny look and chuckled. "We could do that," he agreed. "But we'd both be dying of boredom after two weeks."

A snort escaped me. "True. Maybe we should buy a place somewhere else, a little retreat we can go to whenever we want to escape."

"I like that idea. Should we ask Izzy?"

"Of course. Though I refuse to buy something close to Orlando. The mouse house is not for me. Much too people-y there."

Hardy grinned. "She's more of a Nick channel girl. Unless it's Flynn. Then she's all in."

"Ah, yes. The allure of the smolder. I can see the appeal."

"If you want me to smolder, Dakota, all you have to do is ask." He lifted my hand and kissed the back of it, sending goose bumps racing up my skin.

"Later," I said, waving the notes at him. "We gotta see a guy about a murder first."

ELEVEN

Thankfully, Cole was always easygoing about my random drop-ins. Today, he waved us straight in.

"I know why you're here." He'd been at the dinner last night, but I spotted his blond head only once before being escorted to the back seconds away from a panic attack. I hadn't seen him later on, so I assumed he'd left early.

"Hello to you, too," I said, sinking into the plush chair in front of his desk. Hardy took the other.

"A story took me away last night, but trust me, I heard an earful later from Fletcher." His eyes brimmed with concern. "How's Harper holding up?"

"As well as can be expected. But I think she's getting better. It helps to have a game plan." The faster we solved this, the faster she could put this entire mess behind her.

He reached inside his desk drawer and pulled out a blue folder, pushing it over to me.

"What's this?" I asked, opening it to see a sheath of papers clipped together.

"Everything I have on Harper's boyfriend." His expression turned grim. "Whose name was *not* Aaron Parker."

I pressed my lips together to keep from saying an awful word. The second Harper had told me about him, I had a bad feeling, but it was beginning to look more and more like this guy really was some sort of con man.

The only good thing to come out of this was that Aaron had pulled his last con.

Cole was excellent at research. It would take me at least a couple of hours to go through the packet he provided. "Michael Connor?" I lifted my eyes to Cole.

He nodded. "One of many, though I believe Michael Connor is his birth name. He's taken at least four aliases and left a trail of broken hearts all across the United States. His M.O. is—"

"Hobosexual," I supplied.

Hardy barked a laugh.

Cole's jaw dropped. "Excuse me?"

Hardy rubbed a hand over his mouth, but his eyes gleamed with mirth. "Allow me." He cleared his throat. "It's a term to describe a man with no home who clings to a self-sufficient woman and gaslights her into allowing him to move in and mooch off her."

I blinked. "Close enough."

Cole's lips twitched. "I've been a reporter for as long as I can remember and usually know all the terms way before everyone else learns them. But you got me." He chuckled. "Hobosexual. I'll have to remember that one."

"Let's hope no one you know ever meets one," I said ominously.

Cole's eyes flicked toward the door. Fletcher's office was down the hall, and, despite his intense interest, she had yet to agree to go on a date with him. In fact, she'd cautioned him not to ask her again, and Cole, because he was a good man, had kept his word and his distance. As much as he was able to, with her right down the hall.

I knew what he was thinking. Fletcher was still single. Still dating. Or so he thought. I'd never seen Fletcher go out with anyone in the months I'd known her. She seemed happily single and well-adjusted to a life with no partner. I did my best not to pry, though I suspected whatever this was between them was far from over.

Before I could say anything, his gaze settled back onto me. "I'll do my best to ensure Harper gets a fair shake in the press. I can't make any promises, but this is a small town, and Harper is well-liked. Most people won't believe she's responsible, but there's always a small faction who might stir up trouble."

I sighed. "There always is."

Hardy took the folder and flipped through it, jaw tightening at some of the information listed. We'd have to go through this with a fine-tooth comb when we got back to the office. Sean O'Day might be a good person to have in our corner on this one. Since he was representing Harper, he might have valuable insight and could pick up things we might miss. Having a former detective was already a huge boon for my new business, but having Harper's defense attorney right there with us, receiving information at the same time we did, might speed up our investigation and help clear Harper's name even faster than I hoped.

This was my first murder case as an official private investigator, but it had the potential to be the most important one of my career. For Harper's sake and my own selfish reasons. She was my friend, but she was also the best employee I'd ever had. Of course, the *friend* and the *innocent* part of that was way more important than the other, but if things went sideways, I'd never be able to replace her on either front.

"Is Fletcher in?"

"She's out on a story right now, but I'll tell her you stopped by." Cole hesitated, a look of uncertainty on his face.

"What is it?" I asked.

"I don't really know." His lips tightened. "Something about this case feels different. I'm glad you have Hardy by your side on this one. Be careful."

His concern touched me. "Aww. I didn't know you cared."

Hardy chuckled as he stood tucking the folder under his arm.

"Don't joke," Cole said, his voice more serious than I'd ever heard it. "This guy is obviously a con man, but normally they don't wind up dead. Whoever is responsible was either at your party, involved in the restaurant, or somehow walked into a restaurant full of people and gunned someone down without a single person knowing. It almost feels professional."

His words sent a chill down my spine. "I promise," I said solemnly. "I'll be careful."

Hardy stepped closer. "I agree," he said to Cole. "Something about this does feel different from the normal things Dakota is involved in." He pulled a business card from his wallet. "I don't think you have my new cell number. Give me a call if you find anything else out."

Cole took the card and tucked it into his shirt pocket. "Will do. Please give Harper a hug for me."

"Of course." I went around the desk and reached down to give him a hug. Cole gave me an extra squeeze before letting go.

Hardy nodded to him and led me out of the building, but not before I stopped by Fletcher's office and left her a sticky note telling her to call me. Then I opened her e-mail and sent a note to Cole calling him a fart face.

Seriously. Who left their computer unsecured these days?

Once we were back on the road, Hardy's cell rang. I listened with half an ear as he spoke to someone. When he hung up, he sighed. "That was Paige Monroe. She asked us to do a few more days of surveillance."

There was something in his voice.

"You don't want to?" I probed.

"It's not that." He tapped his fingers on the steering wheel. "She mentioned something odd about the woman he's been seeing. Paige did some digging, and she can't seem to find anything on her."

I frowned. Paige was a lawyer, so she knew how to research. "Is it possible she has the wrong information?"

"Possible. Especially if it's the husband who gave it to her."

"She told him she knows?"

Hardy shrugged. "More than likely not, but he might have let something slip."

"It's a paycheck," I said.

He laughed. "It is. Though I find myself thinking more and more about that discussion we had about buying some land."

"It would be nice to have." I had a lot more time since Harper had taken over more duties and we hired two new people to run the shop. I needed to be busy, but it didn't have to be constant. We could all use a little more relaxation in our lives.

"What do you think about bringing on another investigator?" Hardy asked.

I blinked. "I guess I never thought about it." A laugh escaped me. "Then again, I never thought I'd be in a completely different financial situation than I was when I started expanding the space. I wonder if I still would have done the P.I. firm if I'd come into that money before." The thought sent an uncomfortable feeling through me. Why was I continuing on like everything was normal, when we had the potential to change our lives forever?

Things were changing all around, and I felt frozen in place.

Hardy put his hand on my knee. "I didn't mean to send you into an existential spiral. Let's table this for now and talk about it once we get through these two cases. We have all the time in the world."

I nodded, but my thoughts still swirled. We would both need to keep busy. The fact was ingrained into our DNA. But we didn't have to stress about things. And that might make all the difference for our future.

TWELVE

Izzy flung herself into Fletcher's outstretched arms. "Aunt Fletch!" she cried.

Her exuberance made me grin. Izzy had seen Fletcher only a couple of days ago, but she acted like the woman had gone on a world tour and she hadn't seen her for months.

It solidified my decision that Fletcher was a blessing in my life.

"Aunt Fletch" scooped her up into a hug and stood, Izzy's legs dangling as she clung to her like a leech. "I got hot pizza in there and a recipe to make marshmallow popcorn. Plus...Hocus Pocus!"

Izzy squealed and wiggled for Fletcher to put her down. As soon as her feet touched the ground, Izzy shot into the house like a rocket without saying goodbye to either of us.

Hardy rolled his eyes. "I feel the love."

"It's difficult to resist the siren song of the marsh-mallow popcorn," Fletcher said sagely.

"You bought glitter!" Izzy shrieked from inside the house.

A sheepish smile crossed Fletcher's face. "And glitter."

"Bed by 10," Hardy said.

I elbowed him.

"Thirty," he amended. "Ten-thirty."

One of Fletcher's eyebrows rose.

I elbowed him again.

"Fine. Eleven."

I looked at Fletcher, who still had her eyebrows up.

Hardy snorted. "Eleven-thirty and not a minute more."

"Done," Fletcher said, and backed into her house while waving. "Have fun, Sherlock!"

Hardy grumbled under his breath. "She's going to be so crabby in the morning."

"That's why we leave her with Fletcher until lunchtime. She'll be so tired by the time we pick her up she may take a nap in the car."

He tugged me closer. "I like the way you think, Adair."

"Good. Now let's go catch us a philanderer."

I CONVINCED Hardy to stop one more time for coffee, something he grumbled about but happily did. He tried to convince me to get decaf, but let it drop when I stared at him like he'd grown two heads. Was it even coffee if all the caffeine was gone?

Thanks to a tip from Paige, we sat outside of yet another bar in another bordering town.

"What do you think about going in this time?" Hardy asked.

I glanced at him in surprise. "Do you think we should?"

"I think something about this case is bothering me. I'd like to get a closer look."

The bar was a one-story ramshackle building with a blinking neon sign that said *Shady's*. It looked exactly like it sounded. There was a rickety set of stairs heading up to the entrance, and a few underdressed-for-the-season people loitered there, smoking cigarettes and talking.

I glanced down at my bootcut jeans and mohair sweater. "I won't stick out like a sore thumb?"

Hardy was dressed in a pullover sweater and dark-wash jeans. "We'll just look like a newly married couple looking for a walk on the wild side."

I frowned at him. "That's the exact opposite of what I want."

He grinned. "I know that, but they don't. What do you say? Want to see what Mr. Monroe and his elusive mistress are up to?"

I eyed the bar again. "As long as you take me for a spin around the dance floor."

Hardy turned the car off and slid out. "I'll take you for two."

Music boomed around us the moment we stepped into the place—something from the Top 40 I vaguely recognized. I sidled closer to Hardy, keeping my hand wrapped around his bicep as we headed further in. We got a few funny looks, but overall, people paid us no mind. I think it helped that it was dark and late. Most of the crowd were well into their cups by the time we walked in.

In small towns, things got kicked off much earlier than in the bigger cities. It was past ten, and the place was close to capacity. Hardy took my hand and led me to a small booth at the back of the room. A server was just wiping down the table, so we hovered until she finished. I slid in first and Hardy followed.

"Have you seen him?" I said, speaking into his ear. I could barely hear myself think in this place. There was a reason I never went to bars. If I was going to have a martini, it was with dinner. Never at a place like this.

"Eight o'clock."

I glanced over. He sat with a brunette this time, pretty and thin. But there was a hungry look in her eyes. She never kept her eyes in one place. They darted to and fro, never lighting for more than a couple of seconds on anyone.

"Different girl?" I shook my head. "Mr. Monroe gets around, doesn't he?"

"Maybe," Hardy said, keeping his eyes on our subject. "But they aren't draped all over each other this time."

"You don't think they're together?"

Hardy lifted a shoulder in a shrug. "Not sure." He flagged the server over and ordered two vodka tonics.

"That's going to cost you twenty-five bucks," I said with a laugh.

"Worth it." He draped an arm over the back of the booth. I scooted closer and leaned back to watch.

The server came back with our drinks a few minutes later, dropping off an extra shot glass full of lime. "Ooh. A girl after my own heart," I said. I always put extra lime in my vodka tonics. These were a treat I rarely indulged in, but one wouldn't hurt anyone, and we had to have something in front of us to look normal. Places like these served notoriously awful wine, so Hardy made the right decision when he ordered these.

Nothing happened for a long time. Mr. Monroe and the woman had what looked like an intense conversation before the woman abruptly rose and flounced off. I set my drink down and slid out of the booth.

"Be careful," Hardy said. "I'll wait until you come back before I approach Mr. Monroe." He winked at me. "Otherwise, we'll lose our table."

I pressed the back of my hand against my forehead. "Le swoon."

Hardy's deep chuckle made me laugh.

It wasn't hard to track the woman through the club. She headed straight to the bar and leaned against it, snapping her fingers to get the bartender's attention.

I squeezed in next to her and smiled. "Hey! It's crazy here tonight."

She stared at me for a long moment. "Yeah. It's Ladies' Night. Half price drinks."

"Oh!" I let out a self-deprecating laugh. "It's my first time here. I had no idea."

"Yeah, I can tell." She rolled her eyes and snapped her fingers again.

Ouch. I had to try another tactic. Looking down at myself, I frowned. "It's been a long time since I went out. I just started dating again."

Her gaze flicked to me. "Divorce?"

I nodded. "Ten years married."

She winced. "Kids?"

"Thankfully, no. But getting back out there has been a real nightmare. If this is how dating is, I don't want it."

A hesitant smile crossed her lips. "I feel you."

The bartender was ignoring the woman. If someone snapped at me, I would too. Right now, it was working in my favor.

"You here with anyone?"

She rolled her eyes. "I met up with a guy, but it wasn't a date. Just business."

Business? Hmm. "At a place like this?"

"He owed me some money."

"Ah. Safe place to meet, I guess."

She snorted. "If you say so. Us girls can't be too careful. Especially with guys like him."

"Did he do something to you?"

She waved a hand. The bartender finally headed our way. "Nah. He didn't get the chance." With a look of dismissal, she leaned over and told the bartender what she wanted, then moved a few feet away.

Conversation over, I guess. When the bartender asked what I wanted, I ordered two more vodka tonics and headed back to Hardy with them in hand. Sliding back into the booth, I handed him the other.

He lifted an eyebrow. "Do I need to call a cab?"

"Just to keep up pretenses. I don't plan to drink mine."

"We can write it off."

I'd need to remember that for the future. I wonder if I could claim coffee, too. Oh, the possibilities.

Hardy grinned when he saw my contemplative look. "Monroe hasn't moved from his table. How'd it go with the girl?"

I shrugged. "She said they met for business. Monroe owed her some money."

Hardy tapped his fingers on the table, staring in the direction of the bar. "So she met him here?"

It sounded weird to me, too. "She said girls can't be too careful around guys like him."

Hardy's expression grew thoughtful. "Interesting. All right. Stay here."

"Wait." I reached for him before he slid out of the seat. "Maybe I should do it?"

Hardy tilted his head in confusion.

"We're in a bar. It's a lot less weird for me to approach a man than it is for you."

His expression cleared. "Right. I was thinking like a cop." Sighing, he bent to help me out of the booth. "Be careful. Something about this smells weird."

I agreed. "Back in a minute. When I get back, we're dancing."

Hardy sat back down. "Then we're out of here."

"I like your plan." He winked at me, and I turned away, navigating through the maze of people. The music had shifted into a pulsing techno beat, pounding through my entire body. My teeth rattled with every boom of the drum.

If it were possible, the place had gotten even more crowded. Getting to Mr. Morgan took way longer than I expected, but at last, he came into view. We caught eyes, and a gleam appeared in the watery depths of his gaze.

Gross.

I plastered a friendly smile on my face and pretended I just noticed the open chair next to him. "Oh my gosh! Is this seat taken? Would you mind if I rested for just a little bit?"

His smile sharpened. He stood and held it out for me. "Be my guest, honey."

I was going to have to take twelve showers when I got home.

"Thanks," I breathed, sinking into the sticky seat.

Thirteen showers.

"You want a drink?" Mr. Morgan was a large man. At one time, he must have been in great shape, but time and neglect had taken its toll on his body. His nose, just like his wife had said, was red and dotted with broken capillaries. One of his front teeth was crooked, and his eyebrows were in dire need of a trim.

"I'd love one," I gushed. "Thank you so much." I had zero plans to touch anything that man handled.

He flagged a server down and ordered two beers. Even though he wasn't handling them, I still had an issue taking anything from him. I reached over and stuck my hand out. "Peggy."

He put a clammy hand in mine and shook.

"Derek. What's a stunning woman like you doing in a place like this?"

I shrugged. "I was on a date, but things didn't end so well."

"A date? You single?"

"Newly." I looked away. "I'm trying to get back into the dating game, but it's not so easy."

"Oh, honey. You're a gorgeous little thing. You won't have any trouble."

"What about you?" I lifted my eyes.

His eyes widened with mock surprise. "Me? I'm in that game, too. It's tough out there."

"Oh? Were you on a date tonight, too?"

He shook his head. "Just a business transaction."

I leaned forward and put my hand on top of his, trying not to gag. "What kind of work do you do?"

He leaned in. "Confidential. If I told you, I'd have to kill you."

I giggled. "Like an FBI agent?"

"Nothing like that. I'm an agent of a sort."

"Oh? A sports agent or something?"

He smirked. "Or something. People pay me to find certain things."

"Sounds very mysterious."

He grinned, the dim light making his teeth look artificially bright. "I assure you it is. Maybe one day I'll tell you about it." Derek's eyes shifted away from my face and down to my chest. "It involves affairs of the heart."

Odd thing to say, but Derek was proving to be a strange bird anyway, wasn't he?

I think Paige would have told us if he was an agent of some kind. The way he said it creeped me out. But this wasn't actually what we came here for. There was no evidence of the first blonde woman, and no one else but me had approached him tonight.

"You have plans after this?" he asked.

I clicked my tongue. "I gotta work in the morning. It's going to be an early night, I'm afraid."

"Where do you live?"

I lied through my teeth.

"That's right on my way. I can drive you home if you'd like." He pulled my hand closer and threaded his fingers through mine.

It wasn't even close to where he lived. I tugged my hand away, but Derek didn't want to take no for an answer. He took my hand back. "Don't be shy, honey. If you need a ride, I'm happy to give you one."

A shadow fell over the table. Derek's eyes lifted and flashed with annoyance. "What do you want?" he snapped.

A warm, familiar hand rested on my back. "My girl-friend was just leaving."

An angry smile crossed his lips. "Oh? She said she was single."

Hardy stepped closer. "She was. I've come to beg for her forgiveness." He held out his hand. "You ready?"

I glared at him for a moment. "You have a lot of grov-eling to do, you know."

The edge of Hardy's lip lifted. "Don't I know it. Come on, darling."

I let him lead me away, not looking back at Derek Monroe once. "I'm ready to get out of here," I murmured in his ear.

"Me too," he growled.

But as we made our way to the entrance of the bar, something stopped me in my tracks. A familiar blonde head bobbed along the right side of the club, making a beeline for the middle.

I tugged on Hardy's hand. He frowned, eyes scanning the crowd. When he noticed my target, he stiffened. "What is she doing here?"

I slowly shook my head. "No idea. Let's see where she goes."

Hardy and I were careful to conceal ourselves in the crowd so she wouldn't know she was being followed. When I saw what table she was heading to, my heart dropped to my feet.

Harper took the seat at Derek Morgan's table and pulled

an envelope from her purse, passing it across the table to him. The music obscured everything they said, but Harper's face was drawn and tired, though her eyes snapped with anger. He gave her a mocking smile and rose from the table, leaning down to whisper something in her ear before he walked away.

Hardy tucked me closer. "We should go before she sees us."

"You don't want to ask her why she's here?" I asked in surprise.

"No. We can ask her tomorrow."

Harper dropped her head into her hands and sat there for a moment before she left the table.

Hardy moved farther into the crowd and waited for her to pass by before following.

Once she went outside, we waited a full minute before we left. Hardy peeked out the door to ensure she wasn't watching, motioning for me to follow him. He slung an arm over my shoulder, keeping me closest to the wall of the building as we hurried to our car.

I kept my head down until we were in the car. We were silent for a long moment.

"What the heck?" I finally muttered.

Hardy tilted his head up and let out a long sigh. "This case just got a lot more complicated."

"What was she doing there?" I wondered aloud.

"Whatever it is, Derek is right in the middle of it."

I shuddered. "I never want to talk to that guy again for as long as I live."

"I wanted to smash his head into the table," Hardy snarled.

I blinked and glanced at him, surprised by the vehemence in his tone.

"Hardy?"

His hand flexed against the steering wheel. "There's something about that guy that sends my hackles up. It's not only the cheating and obvious disdain for women. Something is seriously off about him, and I don't want you around him ever again."

My mouth opened and snapped shut. For once, I was at a loss for words. "Okay," was all I could muster after a long pause.

He blew out a breath. "Thank you."

"You don't have to thank me. While I have no intention of being around him again, knowing that it bothers you so much bothers me. I'll let you know if something happens and I have to deal with him again."

He reached over and took my hand. "How about we get out of here?"

"I'm on fourteen showers now."

He gave me a weird look.

"Maybe a good sandblasting, too."

Hardy shook his head. "How about one long, hot shower and a nice, soft bed?"

I thought about it for a moment. "I'll allow it."

THIRTEEN

The bookstore was bustling late the next morning. Hardy and I stopped and bought extra-large coffees on the way. My eyes felt like sandpaper, and my brain was sluggish at best.

"I know I'm not old, but I feel a hundred today," I said as we stepped in.

The newish hire waved at us and continued ringing people up. She was Harper's choice, barely out of high school, and taking community college classes before transferring out to a four-year university. She learned fast and showed up on time, two traits becoming harder and harder to find in many new employees.

"Ditto."

We headed straight to the office to see Sean already there, looking way more chipper and well-rested than we were.

He blinked when he noticed us. "Whoa. Late night?"

Hardy gave a rusty chuckle.

"Surveillance that took an unexpected turn." I handed Sean a coffee. His face lit up.

"Thank you! I was just about to step into the shop and get one, but this is way better. And much bigger."

We set our stuff down and sank onto the couch, both of us focused only on our coffees.

Sean watched us for a minute, grinning, before he returned to his paperwork. "When you've reached appropriate caffeine levels, let me know and we can chat."

Handsome and could read the room? He'd make a good catch for someone. I grunted and sighed when I took the next sip of my coffee.

Hardy grinned at me over the top of the rim of his. He looked just as tired as I was, and it hadn't even been that late when we got home. Maybe 11:30, then we both had to shower, so it was close to one by the time we were both in bed.

I hadn't gone to bed that late in years, and now I remembered why.

Plus, I was sore for some reason. Getting old was a crock.

We sat in silence for the next fifteen minutes, the only sound Sean's pen scratching across the paper.

"I think I'm ready," I finally said.

Sean huffed a laugh and set his pen down. "Welcome to the land of the living."

"I'm not sure I'm there yet, but I can put together some coherent thoughts now."

Hardy held his hand out for my cup. He disappeared into the bookstore while I gathered my notepad and notes from Cole. I still hadn't had the chance to look at them yet, but today was a good day to go through them. Though I had a feeling Hardy and I would be off early today napping, if we could swing it.

Izzy got off at school at 3:30, and it was difficult to nap with a kid in the house, but maybe we could convince her to take one with us.

Sean turned his rolling chair to face me. "I take it this has something to do with Harper?"

"It didn't," I said, "until last night took a weird turn."

His brow furrowed. "Interesting. Should we wait for Hardy?"

The man himself pushed through the doors, holding two more steaming mugs of coffee.

"Gimme," I said.

Hardy set one down in front of me and took the other for himself, settling in at the desk.

"Want to tell him?" I said, reaching for the cup.

Hardy winked. "I'll start."

Thank goodness.

He hit the highlights of the case we were working on for Paige, and Sean didn't interrupt, though I could tell he was wondering how his case and ours had intersected. When we got to the part about Derek, Sean's expression darkened. But it wasn't until we mentioned Harper that Sean threw down his pen and swore.

"She was out? At a bar?!"

Hardy nodded, his expression carefully blank. I stared between them, trying to figure out what I was missing. It came a moment later.

"Oh. Her boyfriend just died. I guess it doesn't look great for her to be out on the town."

Sean snorted. "I'll say! And it's not that he just died. Harper is a murder suspect, and perception is everything." He groaned and rubbed a hand over his face. "I have no idea how I'm going to spin this."

"She gave him an envelope of something," Hardy said.

"And bribery, too?" Sean looked apoplectic. A vein pulsed in his forehead, and his cheeks had turned bright red.

I pressed my lips together to keep from laughing. It wasn't funny, but Harper's poor lawyer looked like he was about to blow a gasket.

Hardy held up a hand. "There's no way to know what was in that envelope."

Sean rolled his eyes and clicked the top of his pen. "What's this Derek guy's last name?"

I told him and also informed him that Paige was a lawyer. His eyes lit up. "Local?"

"Not too far away," I said.

Hardy pulled Paige's card out of his wallet. "Here's her contact information if you want to reach out."

"Awesome." Sean took the card and wrote the info down before handing it back.

"One more thing," I said. "Harper doesn't know we saw her. I'd like to break that news to her if possible."

Sean ripped off the paper and tucked it into his pocket. "Better make it quick. We're meeting for lunch in a couple of hours."

I groaned. There went that pipe dream of a nap.

FOURTEEN

Harper wiped a hand over her eyes. If it were possible, she looked worse than I did today. Her t-shirt was full of wrinkles, and her hair had lost its luster, hanging around her shoulders lifelessly. Dark shadows lurked under her eyes, crescent-moon bruises standing out against her pale skin.

"Want a drink?" I asked.

"Water, please. I'm meeting Sean to go over some case notes after this."

I knew this, but kept my mouth shut. "How are you?"

She lifted a thin shoulder. "Okay, I guess." Harper lifted her hand and chewed on the edge of her thumbnail. I'd never seen her do this before, but Harper wasn't a nervous person, either. "I hate to admit it, but I don't miss Aaron." She dropped her eyes, cheeks flushing with guilt. "Looking back, I can see all the red flags. Now I'm more worried about myself than him. Isn't that awful?"

Empathy swelled in me. I reached across the table and

took her hand. "No. It isn't. You're feeling a very human emotion." I tried to give her a comforting smile. "He wasn't a good person, and you were swept up in his lies. It happens, and it doesn't mean you're to blame. Relief is a common emotion in a situation like this."

A wobbly smile curved her lips. "Thanks, Dakota. You always seem to know the right thing to say."

The server popped by to take our drink order. I got an herbal tea and ordered one for Harper. She protested, but I waved it away. "If you don't want it, I'll drink it. But it's the London Fog blend, so it has lavender." I wiggled my eyebrows. "It's a wonderful nerve tonic."

"I think I need more of a tranquilizer," Harper muttered.

We grinned at each other across the table. As much as I didn't want to ask her this, I knew I had to. Judging people wasn't in my nature. I tried to remain balanced and unbiased, especially when I was looking at clues, but I was close to Harper. I feel like I knew her pretty well, and I couldn't believe she'd be involved in anything sinister or illegal.

If she was, I'd been so wrong about so many things.

Harper's brow furrowed. "Dakota? What's wrong?"

I pulled my hand back and straightened. "I need to ask you about something. If I'm going to help you, I need to know the truth."

Harper stared. "Of course. I've never lied to you."

"Why were you meeting with Derek Morgan last night?"

She sucked on a breath and choked, bending over to cough. The server chose that time to bring our teas and water and set them down as quickly as she could while trying not to stare at Harper.

"You okay?" I asked, when she finally was able to draw a breath.

She took a long sip of water. "Sorry," she said hoarsely. "You surprised me."

She'd done the same thing to me last night. "Hardy and I were there for a case. We saw you come in."

Harper sighed and looked away. "You're going to think I'm a fool."

I shook my head. "Never. I promise."

She frowned. "Wait. How do you know who Derek Morgan is? Is he who you're surveilling?"

"I can neither confirm nor deny."

"I'll take that as a *yes*. The guy is a total creep."

"And you were meeting with him, why?" I probed.

"He runs the speed dating thing—Speeding for Love."

I tried not to wince. That was a terrible name.

"It's not open to the public. I had to be recommended by a current member to become a member. Very exclusive. Very hush-hush."

I was getting a bad feeling about this. "Okay. Very expensive?"

She nodded. "This was the third and final installment payment. Normally, I pay the main woman, but Derek reached out to me and asked me to meet him for the last payment."

I pulled out my notebook. "What's the woman's name?"

"Lucy." Her eyes narrowed. "I can't remember her last name. Maybe Horn?"

I jotted it down and put a question mark after Horn. "What does she look like?"

Harper looked up, lost in thought. "Small. Brunette. Thin. She has a sharp face."

I wrote everything down. That description fit a lot of people in town, but I felt like she was important.

"Did you know about Derek before he called you?" I asked.

She shook her head. "It was always Lucy. She's the one who reached out to me after the friend recommended me."

"Who's the friend?" I was starting to think this was no friend at all.

"Her name is Markie. I don't know her last name."

Don't judge. Don't judge. I kept my face blank. "And what does she look like?"

"Blonde. Short. Her hair is curly and frizzy."

I wrote that down, too. "Does your lawyer know all of this?"

Harper shook her head, cheeks coloring again. "He doesn't know about the speed dating thing." She paused. "Well. He knows I met first met Aaron at an event, but he doesn't know I paid for it or anything."

"It might not matter, but I'll let him know since he's working in our office now."

"Thanks." She twisted her hands together over and over. I'd never seen her this fidgety, and it worried me.

"Harper?"

She looked up.

"It's going to be okay. We're working hard to find out who did this."

Her smile didn't reach her eyes. "I know." She took a sip of her tea, grimaced, and pulled the sugar over.

"Can you tell me how much the speed dating cost?"

"Too much," Harper said, shaking her head in disgust. "Two grand. They work with you until you make a good match and then guarantee it for six months."

My eyebrows rose to my hairline. "Two thousand?"

"It's just I've tried so hard to find someone, and it never works out—"

"Harper. You don't have to justify anything to me. Ever. I'm worried about you. That's all. I don't get to say how you spend your money or tell you how to live your life." But something was bothering me. "This may sound callous, but since Aaron was a disaster, did you ask for your money back?"

Harper let out a burst of genuine laughter. "Oh, I wish! They have a three-strikes policy."

That sent me into a fit of giggles. "I feel like Aaron should count for three."

Harper cackled, and suddenly, the world righted itself. Everything would be okay. We'd find out who was responsible for this and take them down.

Harper was going to be okay.

FIFTEEN

I kissed Izzy on the nose and tucked her in with her favorite sheep stuffed animal.

"I love you, Dakota," Izzy murmured, before she rolled onto her side and closed her eyes.

I froze like a deer in the headlights, tears springing to my eyes. I opened my mouth, closed it, then shut my eyes and took a deep breath. I had everything now. My life was complete.

I sank onto the edge of her bed, stroked a hand through her hair, and leaned down to kiss her on the temple. "I love you too, my little darling."

When I rose, it was on shaky legs, and I had to use the wall to steady myself.

Hardy stood at the door, tears shimmering in his eyes as well.

We stepped out into the hall, quietly shutting Izzy's door.

In one graceful move, Hardy turned me and gently pushed me against the wall, sliding his lips over mine.

When we came up for air, he pressed his forehead to mine. "You've given me everything I ever could have wanted, Dakota."

I shook my head. "That was my line."

We quietly laughed before he took my hand and led me to the couch. I reached for the notebook with Harper's case notes, but Hardy stayed my hand. "Not tonight. Let's just...bask for a little while."

I snuggled into his side. "Can you believe that?" I asked after a while.

"Of course I can. If she loves you even a tenth of how much I do, she's liable to burst with it."

I snorted. "Flatterer."

"You've given my little girl her life back, Dakota. If I didn't love you before, I would have fallen in love with you then. Instead, it only made me fall harder."

I swallowed. "She's amazing. I promise I will do my absolute best to be the mother she deserves." Izzy didn't call me Mom, and I didn't expect her to. I'd be whatever she needed me to be.

We sat there in the quiet for a while, basking in the marvels and joy a few little words could make, before we called it a night and headed to bed.

Harper's case was important, but tonight, we took a much-needed break.

We felt a lot more human the next day and popped into the office bright and early. Sean, once again, was already there. I wondered if it would be weird to have a third party we didn't know working there temporarily, but Sean had managed to fit into our lives seamlessly.

Odd, but Fletcher had done the same thing, and now we were fast friends. Maybe it was something in the family genes.

He greeted us with a friendly wave.

"I do not know how you can be so chipper every single morning," I said.

Hardy grinned at him as he came around the side. "Don't mind Dakota. She's always grumpy before 9 a.m."

"I am not!" I said hotly.

Hardy lifted a brow. "Of course not, darling."

His dry delivery made me belly laugh. I guess I *was* a little grumpy in the mornings, wasn't I?

"I didn't know what time you planned on coming in, but next time coffee is on me," Sean said.

Hardy waved the words away. "No worries. We try to come in the mornings, but our schedule is always a little erratic."

"I'll catch you one day," Sean said with a smile. "But I'm glad you're here, regardless. Harper and I met yesterday. I don't have much news, but I did get a full work up on the victim." He reached into his desk and pulled out a folder. "I have permission from Harper to share information from her case, but I have a document I'll need you to sign if you don't mind. It's a standard NDA."

Hardy took the sheet of paper he offered and perched

on the edge of the couch as he read over it. He nodded to me. "Nothing concerning. Got a pen?"

Sean laughed. "Fletcher would have my hide if I tried anything." At my look, he said, "Not that I would! Fletch and I were raised right. Our mother would tan our hides if we did anything dishonorable."

Hardy gave him an incredulous look. "So you became a lawyer?"

Sean rubbed his thumb and fingers together. "Money." His eyes sparkled with amusement. "We're from a poor Irish family, and I swore I'd make something of myself so I could take care of Mom and Fletch."

"I bet Fletcher loved that," I said dryly.

Sean grinned. "Yeah, she threatened to hog-tie me and throw me in the river if I ever implied she needed help."

"Sounds about right."

"She's calmed down now," he added. "Now if we go out to dinner, she claims she's a lowly reporter and I'm a big city lawyer and I should be the one to pay."

"That sounds like her, too." Hardy handed me the pen and paper. I took the time to read over it, too. I trusted Hardy, but I always read every document in its entirety before I signed.

Once I confirmed it was a standard NDA, I signed and handed both back to Sean.

"Great." He clapped his hands together. "Now we're officially in business."

"We have news, too," I said. "But you go first. Tell me what they have on Harper and how things are looking."

His eyes darkened. "Not good, I'm afraid. She had motive, means, and opportunity."

At my outraged look, he shook his head. "At least according to the police."

"They've known her for years!" I blurted out.

"They're looking at the evidence," Hardy said. "We have to treat every suspect equally in a case. Harper is no exception."

"She should be," I muttered, knowing he was right but not liking the fact that Harper was being treated the same as everyone else. I straightened. "Wait. Every suspect?" I looked at Sean. "Are there more?"

"Turn of phrase," Hardy said.

But Sean nodded. "There are a couple of people on their radar. But they have more on Harper than the others."

At Hardy's intense interest and tight jaw, Sean snorted. "A good lawyer always has info sources in law enforcement. We have to if we want to do the best job for our clients."

Hardy drew in a deep breath and gave a stiff nod. "All right. I'm no longer an officer so I'll let it go, but a leak in the department is a concern for everyone."

I chimed in. "But helpful for us."

Hardy's dark look made me look down to keep from laughing.

"Anyway," Sean said, "let's get this train back on the track. She has an uphill battle ahead of her if we can't find the real culprit. If she has to go to trial..." He trailed off. "Well. Let's hope we don't have to."

On that grim note, I had to tell him something else. "Harper was paying a company for dating services. Speed dating, to be specific." I glanced down at my notes. "Speeding for Love is the place. They set up these events for interested people and are supposed to screen for quality. Harper said they guarantee a match and offer refunds if the match doesn't last more than six months."

Sean blinked. "And Aaron slipped through?"

Hardy's expression turned thoughtful. He tapped his fingers on the edge of the couch. "What if Aaron was supposed to slip through?"

Sean's eyes narrowed. "You mean they purposely put people like him into the dating pool to...what? Bilk vulnerable women?"

My heart hurt for Harper. "She paid two grand to participate and said she had to be recommended for the program. A woman named Markie got her in."

Sean sucked air through his teeth. "Two grand?"

I sat down at my desk and pulled my keyboard over, typing in the web address. It brought up a flashy, graphics-heavy site with very little info. "Speeding for Love has a fancy website, but I can't see much without a membership. There's an access code to get in and a referral code." A thought occurred to me. "Two grand is a drop in the bucket, but we need a referral code from someone using the service."

Hardy and I locked gazes. "Harper," we said at the same time.

A COUPLE OF HOURS LATER, we had both codes. Sean and Hardy stood behind me while I typed both in. A pop-up screen appeared, displaying a long wall of text. When I tried to bypass it, the site beeped at me.

"Terms and conditions," Sean said, leaning over me to study the document. "If you scroll too fast, it will make you read it again. I'd recommend waiting a minute and then scrolling to the bottom. It should time out and let you through."

"Should I read all this?" It made me feel icky not to read the TOS, but I was using a false name and a fake e-payment account I'd set up on the fly. Hardy had a credit card tied to an inheritance trust that couldn't be traced back to either of us. It might flag suspicion later on, but we doubted it would be an issue for at least a week or two. Or until we started causing trouble.

Once I agreed to the terms, I paid the two grand, and it led me to an events page with pictures of the next speed-dating participants. I scrolled down, skimming to see if I knew anyone, but there wasn't a single familiar face among them.

"If this place is local, wouldn't we know more partici-pants?" Hardy asked.

"Harper never said where she was when she met him. I'd think it wouldn't be too far out of the way, but it is odd that we don't recognize anyone here. Not that I know everyone in town, but I know most people." I glanced back at him. "I'd venture to guess you know more people than I do. You don't recognize anyone here?"

Hardy peered closer. "Scroll up, please."

We went through the entire site. Hardy shook his head. "No one." He frowned. "Right click on one of the pictures and search Google."

I did as he asked, choosing a woman named Samantha, who was 26 and supposedly from Silverwood Hollow. A bunch of images popped up, including the same exact picture on the dating site, but this time, the picture connected to a social media account.

"See if her account is public," Hardy said.

I clicked on the picture.

"Roslyn Matthews," I read.

Sean pulled a chair over and sat down. "Age 29. No location or occupation listed. Scroll through her feed, please."

We went through the last year of social media posts. Her profile wasn't public, so we didn't glean much, only some profile picture changes and the occasional group tag. "The profile doesn't look fake, does it?"

"No, but it's not difficult to fake this kind of thing. Depending on how long they've been running this con, they might have a bunch of people running social media accounts." Sean scribbled furiously in his notebook. "Mind clicking over to the dating site again?"

Sean chewed on the side of his lip. "Mind if I grab the mouse?"

"Sure." I rolled my chair over to give him some room.

Sean clicked a few things, then went to the Events page. "Huh."

I didn't see anything.

"There's only Silverwood Hollow listed. Nowhere else. That's interesting."

"So there's no way to tell who the other participants are in other cities," Hardy said. "What are the odds they're using the same people over and over again?"

Sean kept flipping back and forth from page to page. "I don't understand how this works," I said. "Harper told me there was a no-refund policy once the match lasted longer than six months. So why would they use the same people for this?"

"It's a long con." Hardy pulled a chair over and sat beside me, stretching his long legs out. "What's six months with someone when you can spend it bilking them out of their life savings?"

I swallowed hard. "Is that what he did to Harper?"

Sean muttered something under his breath before saying, "No. He got some money out of her by way of living for free under her roof, but she drew the line at funding any business expenses or ventures. I know she paid for gas and other smaller things, but I think her savings are still intact."

"Except for the two grand she spent on this scam." I rubbed my eyes. Frustration made me antsy. I wanted to go find everyone involved in this and send them to jail for a very, very long time.

"She can get a refund, right?" Sean asked. "Aaron wasn't around for six months."

I laughed. "I said the same thing to Harper. You wouldn't believe what they told her."

"Oh, I bet I would," Sean grumbled.

"She has to give it three full rounds, then they'll give her the money back."

Sean burst out laughing. He rubbed his hands together like a kid in a candy store. "I am so going to enjoy bringing these clowns down."

I sat up ramrod straight. A kernel of an idea was forming. "How about a speed dating event at my store?"

"It wouldn't work," Hardy said. "We're combined with a P.I. firm. They wouldn't bite."

"Hmm." I tapped my fingers on the desk. "What about a Books and Beaus event hosted somewhere other than Tattered Pages? I can sponsor it, but we can host it at a coffee shop or café."

Sean was nodding his head. "I like it. If none of these people are from Silverwood, they won't recognize you. I'd recommend disguising your hair and maybe your eye color and actually participating in the event."

"No," Hardy barked.

"She's perfect for this," Sean argued. "Plus, she's a paid-up member, so she has access the rest of us won't be able to get."

Hardy's eyes glittered with anger. "It's too dangerous. We won't know what she's walking into."

"It's a speed-dating event. Since none of them are from here, the participants won't know who I am. I can see how they run the thing and see if there's anything fishy about it."

"And we all know there's something fishy about it," Sean added.

"Maybe I can see if I can recommend Fletcher. She'd love to do something like this." A story like that would be right up her alley.

When Sean flinched, Hardy laughed. "Not so keen on turning your sister loose on this, but it's okay for my wife to do it?"

I froze. He called me his wife. Warm fuzzies spread from my head to my toes. I'd marry that man right now if he would let me.

Sean had the grace to look chagrined. "You're right. I still think it's the best way to get close to it. And I can't tell Fletcher anything. If she wants to do it, she will." He let out a rueful laugh. "If I tried to tell her no, she'd bite my head off."

"Just like Dakota is about to do to me," Hardy said with a sigh. I don't think he realized what he had just called me.

"I think it's one of the safer things I can do," I said. "Nothing has happened at any of the events. Harper was with the guy for at least a few weeks before anything happened."

"Anything meaning him being dead," Hardy said.

I scooted closer to him. "We're private investigators. This is our job."

He shut his eyes for a moment before giving me a sharp nod. "I know. But I want to always be the one who walks into danger. Not you."

"We're partners. We have to share the burden."

"You two are so sweet," Sean said in a saccharine voice.

"I'm definitely asking Fletcher to come with me," I shot back. "Get ready for a new scammer brother-in-law. I hope his name is Harry, and he brings over a big dog that sheds everywhere."

Hardy's deep laugh broke the tension.

"It's settled then. I'm going to the next event, which is in..."

Sean flipped back to the events screen. "Two days. Wednesday evening."

"Good. I'll go to this one and see about setting another one up. The event this week might not shed a lot of light on their internal workings, but if they allow me to host one soon, I think I'll get a lot more info about where the money is going, or at least meet some of the people in charge."

"I'll feel better if we can do a more thorough disguise than just hair and eye color," Hardy said.

"Fletcher is excellent with disguises. She did quite a bit of undercover work at her last job." Sean made some additional notes and passed the mouse back over to me.

"Then I think we're all set," I said.

"Oh goodie," Hardy drawled.

SIXTEEN

The speed-dating site was ecstatic about the opportunity to host another event. We scheduled another one a week after tonight's event. I contacted the new coffee shop, and they were happy to host on such short notice. Such was the beauty of a small town.

We agreed on a rate to reserve the place after hours, and I contacted Harper to let her know.

"Oh! Can I decorate the place?" she asked.

"I—what? You want to be involved?"

She snorted. "Of course I do. Whatever I can do to clear my name, I am game. Plus, I feel like I'm going stir-crazy. I want to come back to work, but I know it's not a good idea right now. Sean was really mad about the bar thing, and I've been cautioned not to be out and about too much until this is over."

"I'm not worried about you going back to the store. Tattered Pages will be fine. If you want to work, I'll add you back to the schedule. I pulled you off to give you a while to grieve and get things in order for your case, but if you're ready, I'm happy to change it."

"You're the best boss a girl could ever have," Harper said quietly. "Keep me off for now. I know you say it will be all right, but I love Tattered Pages as much as you do, and I think my presence will be a distraction. Let's see how the next week goes. After that, we can talk about it."

I couldn't imagine how she felt. When I first got involved in cases, I had a couple where the spotlight fell on me, but it was never as serious as Harper's case.

"Let me know if you change your mind."

"I will. But back to the decorating. Can I do it?"

I glanced at the unfinished window. Harper and Izzy had never finished it before everything happened. "Of course you can. I'd suggest you come as early as possible and leave before the event starts, though. Just so no one will think you're participating."

"That's a good point. I'll make sure I'm out of there as soon as possible."

"One more thing."

"Hmm?"

"How about you pop by the store and finish up our window? It will be good to get out, and you know I'm not nearly as excited about decor as you are."

The line fell silent for a long moment.

"I'd like that. Tomorrow?"

"Day after. I have no idea how tonight will go, and I might be zapped tomorrow. Come by once the shop is closed. I'll bring Izzy and Hardy, and I'll call Daniel and Fletcher. We'll make it a pizza party or something."

"That sounds amazing." I could hear the smile in her voice.

"It's a date, then. Take care." Just as I was about to hang up, Harper spoke again.

"Dakota?"

"Yes?"

Harper hesitated. "Be careful," she said after a moment. "My events were always safe, but this Aaron thing has me on edge."

"I'm always careful. But just to be sure, Hardy will be waiting for me in the parking lot."

"Oh good. All right. I'll see you in a couple of days."

We hung up. Hardy helped me into my jacket, and we were off.

"I don't like this," Hardy said for at least the third time. "Plus, I like that dress. I wish you wouldn't wear it tonight."

I gave him a bemused smile. "I'll buy a new one so we can make new memories."

"You better not have any fun," he grumbled, as he pulled into the parking lot of the restaurant.

I put my hand over my heart. "I solemnly swear to have a miserable time."

Hardy chuckled. "I'll hold you to that."

We arrived an hour early to avoid notice. Cole pulled in behind us and waved. I leaned over and kissed my fiancé, murmuring to him that I'd be home by eleven, and hurried out of his vehicle into Cole's. We couldn't risk anyone seeing Hardy, just in case he was recognized.

Cole had the seat heater turned on. I groaned when I got in, pulling my shawl closer. "Thanks for doing this."

His green eyes looked like they glowed in the low light. "Are you kidding? I'd be wounded if you failed to invite me to participate in your shenanigans, especially if I know how grumpy Hardy's going to be about it."

I laughed. "You know him too well."

"I'm sure he's a bubbling cauldron of rage," Cole said, as he grinned and waved at Hardy. My fiancé gave him a dark look before whipping the vehicle out of the parking lot. He'd be back when the event started and not a moment before that.

"Be nice."

Cole grinned. "You look completely different, by the way. It's a little startling."

I fluffed my fake hair. "Thank you. I joined the site using false credentials. You have no idea how hard it is to get a fake license to pass muster these days."

He shook his head. "From bookseller to private eye. I never thought I'd see the day." Cole reached over and tugged a blonde curl. "I like it. Sometimes dark-haired women can't go blonde without it looking weird, but it looks good on you."

I eyed him. "Are you moonlighting as a hairstylist or something? Why do you know so much about hair color?"

"I've interviewed a lot of women in my day."

"Which answers zero of my questions." He was right,

though. I'd chosen a curly, dirty-blonde wig with brunette lowlights. The new hair color forced me to change my makeup, and that was a little bit of a challenge until Fletcher had come over last night and showed me how to cool things down. Then she dragged me out of the house and took me shopping.

We'd come back with two outfits: a dark-green wrap dress and a red skirt with an off-the-shoulder top. Hardy had said nothing, but I saw his jaw tighten when I put on the red skirt, so I'd chosen to wear the green dress. I don't think it would have mattered what I'd put on. He did not want me to go, and wouldn't want me to wear anything even remotely flattering.

His jealousy was cute, but it got a little grating as the night had worn on, until he'd finally groaned, apologized to both of us, and stalked out of the room.

He was a little better today, but I didn't think he'd be 100 percent until I was back in his car, safe and sound.

"We got an hour," Cole said. "Want to listen to a podcast?"

"Nothing about murder, please."

"You got it. Let's learn about finances, then."

"Cole. Please don't put me to sleep before 9 p.m. I have twenty-five dates to get through tonight."

He snickered as he picked up his phone and started sorting through things to listen to.

This was going to be a long night.

Fifteen minutes later, a black van with the Speed Dating for Love logo pulled into the parking lot. We were fortunately not the only vehicle there. The restaurant employees were still inside, so Cole and I ducked down to avoid their notice as they began unloading.

I spotted two men, but I couldn't see who was on the passenger side, and I had to be careful about being seen.

We waited until they were walking up the steps to the restaurant before we popped our heads up. There were two additional women with them, but all I could see were the backs of their heads.

"When I leave, I'll grab the tags off the van and send them to Hardy," Cole said.

"Thanks." I let out a deep, cleansing breath.

"Nervous?"

"I've never been speed-dating before."

He laughed. "It must be weird to date right before your wedding," he said dryly.

I grinned and pulled out my cell to send Hardy a quick message before I went inside.

"You have your mic on?" Cole asked.

I tapped the small pin on my shawl. Hardy had access to some cool toys. "Right here."

"When's Fletcher supposed to be here?"

"Fifteen minutes before it starts."

Cole nodded, the slight tightening of his jaw telling me exactly how he felt about Fletcher's participation in this madness. I decided to poke the bear a little bit.

"I'm not worried about tonight. Fletcher is going to be the hot ticket this evening. She'll probably walk out with a dozen numbers."

"I know what you're doing, you succubus."

"Oh?" I adopted an innocent tone. "What am I doing? Am I wrong?" I batted my eyelashes at him.

His dark look made me grin. "I haven't asked her out again," he growled.

"Women like a man who respects their boundaries."

"I should move on," he said.

I thought about it. Fletcher didn't talk about Cole much, and she refused to engage when I tried to bring it up gently. My intuition told me she liked him, but I didn't know why she refused to let anything happen between them.

"If you think it's best," I said, trying to stay neutral. "You don't have to ask her out on a date, but have you ever thought about trying to spend more time with her?"

He glanced at me. "We work together. I see her every day."

"Not like that. I see the new hires almost every day, but it doesn't mean I spend time with them. How about picking up lunch for her and eating together at the desk or outside at the picnic tables? Or I dunno, saying you need some help picking out a suit and ask her to go with you."

Cole's expression turned thoughtful.

"Try to be her friend first. Don't go into expecting anything, though. That will screw it up before it even gets off the ground. Have no expectations and try to enjoy the ride. Don't push her boundaries but be there...available. Get to know her."

Cole nodded slowly. "I like that idea."

I lifted a shoulder in a shrug. "Sometimes I have good ones."

"You mentioned her brother was working in the office with you?"

"Yes. Sean. I like him. He won't be with us forever, but it's kind of cool having new blood in the office. Hardy likes him, too."

"Is he like her?"

"Fletcher?" I shook my head. "Not really. Ice and fire are a good way to describe them, I think. He's not cold, but he's steady. Fletcher, as you know, is a little feisty."

A fond smile curved his lips. "I do."

We chatted for a while longer until I spotted Fletcher's car pulling into the parking lot. Cole straightened and ran a self-conscious hand over his hair.

When he caught me looking, he glared, making me laugh. "Don't you dare say a word."

I mimed zipping my lips and waited for Fletcher to come to the car.

She tapped on the window a minute later and leaned down when Cole lowered it.

"Hey."

Cole cleared his throat. "Hey."

I leaned over and waved. "You ready to go a-dating?"

Fletcher rolled her eyes. "I had to put on lipstick for this. It better be good. You ready?"

I nodded. "Born ready."

"Be careful," Cole said. "Both of you."

"I'd eat these men for breakfast," she shot back.

Cole's eyes widened.

Shaking my head, I slid out of the car, adjusting my shawl around my shoulders, carefully keeping the pin at my collarbone.

"Show time," Fletcher murmured, locking elbows with me as we walked inside.

SEVENTEEN

An attendant stopped us when we got to the hostess stand. She was short, blonde, and had blinding white teeth, bared in a smile reminiscent of the home shopping channel. The woman held a clipboard and a pen and wore a pink suit with a cream-colored camisole and matching high heels.

"Hello!" she chirped. "I'm Charity! Welcome to Speed Dating for Love!"

Every sentence ended with an excited punch. Fletcher gently elbowed me.

"This is a private event tonight, ladies. I'm assuming you're members?"

"We are," Fletcher said.

"Wonderful!" She consulted her clipboard. "And what is your name?" she asked Fletcher.

"Genevieve O'Shea."

Charity skimmed down to the O's. "There you are!" She made a checkmark on the paper and picked up a small yellow envelope. "Here's the packet for new members." She handed that off and picked up a pre-printed name tag. "And if you'll wear this, we'd greatly appreciate it! The name tag helps potential matches during the event." She leaned in closer. "And they'll make a point of remembering it if they want to get to know you a little better." Charity winked. "If you know what I mean."

"Yes," Fletcher said faintly. "The wink gave it away."

Charity's brilliant smile flickered a hair. "And you!" She turned to me. "Who do I have the pleasure of speaking with tonight?"

"Addie Parker."

"P. P. Parker," Charity murmured as her perfectly manicured finger slid down the paper. "There you are! Welcome to you, too!" She handed me the same items. "There are plenty of people already in there just waiting to meet you two beautiful gals! The cocktail hour is upon us, so feel free to have a drink or two and loosen up."

"Are we stiff?" Fletcher asked.

I elbowed her this time.

"Excuse me?" Charity said, that toothpaste-commercial smile flickering again.

"I'm just kidding!" Fletcher said, a brilliant grin lighting up her face. "But boy, do I need a drink. What a day!"

Charity nodded enthusiastically. "Great! Thanks so much for choosing our company to service your dating needs!"

I dragged Fletcher away.

"Ugh. Gross," Fletcher whispered. "If the Stepford Wives came to life, she'd be the poster child."

I laughed under my breath. "Let's try to be a little less sassy to the participants, please."

"Yes! Of course! Anything you say!" Fletcher's voice was a spot-on mimic of Charity's high-pitched enthusiasm.

Rolling my eyes, I steered her toward the bar. I'd need at least one drink to get through this night.

I was glad I invited Fletcher. All eyes were on her, leaving me to nurse a drink and hold up the wall. She had a natural charm about her, even if every single thing out of her mouth was a lie. Fletcher cast a spell on the men who dared approach her, gently rebuffing any requests for a phone number "until the event was over because everyone deserves a fair shake."

She was a snake charmer, hypnotizing every single person who got close enough to hear her music. I'd never seen anything like it.

If Cole managed to land her, he'd have his hands full.

But the even more amazing thing about her was that she was never inappropriate or rude. When someone got a little too pushy, she manipulated them with the skill of a big-shot lawyer, sending them away with a smile and a slightly dazed look.

By the end of the night, she'd have every single man in here eating out of her hand.

On the flip side, we might need a police escort out, if the heated glares from some of the women were anything to go by. Fletcher was the center of attention, and not in a good way.

"Don't go to the bathroom by yourself," I murmured when we were finally alone.

"Oh, I see them," she whispered. "Those glares are hot enough to set me on fire."

"Maybe you should tone down the annoying natural charm?" I said wryly.

Fletcher's eyes widened. "It's the Irish in me. We can't help but charm the pants off of every man we meet."

"Maybe just keep the charm low enough to where they keep their pants on, please."

She held up her hands. "I make no promises."

"Two vodka tonics, please. Extra lime," I said to the bartender, who was listening to our conversation and trying not to smile.

"Coming right up."

"I've never had one of those," Fletcher mused.

"I didn't want to give you the chance to order because I need to walk out of here on my own two feet."

She grinned. "It's the Irish again."

"Yeah. Well, the Irish need to cool it."

The bartender laughed out loud.

Fletcher grinned. "See. He knows."

"He's a bartender. Of course he wants us to drink."

He set our drinks in front of us. "I'm already paid up for the drinks, but a tip wouldn't be amiss."

"Open bar?" Fletcher asked, as she picked up her drink.

"Until eleven." He leaned closer. "You two new here?"

We both nodded.

"Thought so. Be careful. They ask us to make the drinks extra strong."

I stared dubiously at my vodka tonic.

"Don't worry. I made them normal for you two."

Fletcher gasped in dismay.

"I'll get you next time if you want it, doll," he said. "These guys want everyone's inhibitions lowered. The more matches they make, the more money they get."

"You work bar for them often?" I asked, squeezing the extra limes and smushing them into the glass.

"Local area, yes. From what I understand, they travel all over the country." He straightened and gave us a vague smile. "Have a nice night, ladies."

My brow furrowed.

"And how are you two doing?" an annoyingly chipper voice said. "Is everything going well?"

I turned and saw a familiar dark-haired woman standing there. She wore a name tag that said *Lucy*. My heartbeat spiraled into a frenzy. This was the woman who met Derek at the bar. How were those two connected?

My hair was a different style and color. I'd done my makeup wildly different and had applied self-tanner liberally. I was wearing different colored contacts and dressed drastically differently than how I looked at the bar. Plus, it had been dark and loud, and the woman had not wanted to talk to me. This would be the test of how well my disguise would stand up to her scrutiny.

"Everything is great," Fletcher gushed, forcing Lucy's attention away from me and onto her. "And having an open bar? What a divine idea."

Lucy blinked, her eyes widening as she got a good look at Fletcher. "Er. Well. Good. I'm happy to hear that. This is your first time here?"

Fletcher nodded. "We just got here a little while ago and haven't had the chance to mingle, but we're about to start!" She shook the ice in her drink a little. "What time do the official events start?"

"Twenty minutes," Lucy said faintly.

Fletcher let out a little squeal. "This is so exciting!"

I pressed my lips together to keep from laughing out loud. If Fletcher ever wanted a new job, I'd hire her as a P.I. in a heartbeat. Maybe I should bring it up to her. Lucy hadn't even given me a second glance since Fletcher got ahold of her.

"Yes, well. I must greet everyone else this evening, but I'm glad to see you're settling in well." This Lucy was wildly different from the Lucy at the bar. She was dressed more conservatively, wearing a pair of stovepipe pants, high heels, and a silky blouse. Her makeup was toned down, and her hair twisted in a neat chignon. Lucy looked like she'd be right at home in a high society luncheon.

"Thank you!" Fletcher called, waving frantically as Lucy made her escape.

"I'll give you a double next time," the bartender drawled. "Well done."

Fletcher winked at him and pulled me by the arm and into the sea of people. "Let's go mingle, Addie."

When we were out of earshot, I quietly said, "If you ever want to start a new career, I'd love to have you on board. I had no idea you could lie that well."

Fletcher's eyes crinkled around the edges. "It's part of being a reporter. We lie in the beginning so we can tell the truth later."

"You're probably excellent at sneaking into places."

"It's a combo of the red hair and my silver tongue."

I couldn't help but laugh. "The offer is on the table. We'll pay you well, and give you all the leeway you want, as long as you stay within the parameters of the law." I thought about it for a moment. "Or, if you skirt that line, don't tell Hardy."

Fletcher snorted. "He is a pretty straight-laced man, isn't he?"

"He has his moments that surprise me."

"Three o'clock," Fletcher murmured, slapping a smile on her face. "Hello!"

A tall man with a gleam in his eyes stood about a foot away from us. His name tag said Tom. "Hello, you two." He spoke to both of us, but he only had eyes for Fletcher.

"Hello," I said politely.

"Sooo," the man drawled, "is this your first time?"

"It sure is. The dating game is rough, so I thought I'd try something new. You?"

Tom chuckled. "No. I've been a few times, but no luck so far." He shrugged and sipped an amber liquid from his glass. Probably an Old Fashioned. He looked like the kind to drink something like that. He wore a pair of chinos and a crisp white t-shirt with loafers. No socks. His jawline was sharp and peppered with five o'clock shadow. Dark, well-styled hair and light brown eyes, sharp nose...the guy was handsome, but there was something I didn't like about him, and I couldn't put my finger on it.

Fletcher tilted her head and studied him. "I'm surprised by that. Why do you think nothing has clicked for you?"

His smile sharpened. "Because you weren't here."

Gag.

Fletcher's eyes widened before she laughed, but I could tell the difference between her fake laugh and her real one. This poor guy didn't stand a chance. "Clever," she said. "Trite, but clever."

Tom's smile faltered. He wasn't sure if she'd insulted him or not. "I try." He laid a hand over his chest and bowed his head slightly. "Why do you think you haven't found anyone?"

Fletcher lifted a shoulder in a careless shrug. "I'm very choosy."

"Oh?" Tom's interest piqued. "In what way?"

"I wish to have a partner. Picking up after someone isn't something that interests me. I want someone who sees something in the house that needs to be done and does it."

Tom's interest waned. "Is that so?"

Fletcher's smile turned predatory. "It is. You don't seem to like that, Tom. Why is that? Are you the kind of guy who'll walk right past a pile of dirty dishes and ignore them because you know your wife will do them?"

"I—I wouldn't say that."

"Then what would you say?"

I put a warning hand on her arm. We couldn't antagonize the men too much. His attention shifted to me, and I saw the moment he decided to switch targets. "What about you?"

Fletcher's huff of laughter almost made me smile, but I managed to project an air of gullibility. "What about me?"

"Do you like doing the dishes?" Tom asked.

Saints alive. What kind of people was Lucy inviting to these things? "Does anyone like doing dishes?" I asked.

"A necessary evil," Fletcher interjected.

I nodded. "Yes. Having dirty dishes lying around is stressful."

Tom studied me. "What kind of partner are you looking for?"

I knew I should be good, but I couldn't help myself. "Preferably one who does the dishes sometimes."

Tom sighed and tilted his drink. "Nice chatting with you ladies. Have a good evening."

We waited until he was out of hearing range before Fletcher snorted. "Eww."

"They can't all be like that, can they?"

"I'm not here to date anyone, but if they are, this might be unbearable."

Music struck up then, bringing the noise down to a

quiet murmur. Lucy appeared on the stage. Applause rang out, along with cheers and whistles.

"Hello, hello!" she said, her voice amplified through a mic she wore at her cheek. "Welcome to Speed Dating for Love!"

More raucous applause. Had we walked into a cult? The entire vibe of this felt off.

"Each round will go four minutes. When you hear the sound of the bell, get up and head to your next match! But before you do, ensure you fill out your paper with a *yes* or *no* and drop it in the jar! That will allow us to tabulate all your matches at the end."

More cheers.

Lucy's too-white smile was blinding in the artificial light. "We will go for an hour and a half. At the end, we will quickly calculate matches. Those who don't have any matches—"

Boos rang out.

Lucy stuck her bottom lip out. "Will have to go home. Those left who have matches will do one more round to narrow their selections down to their top three!"

Okay. The cheers were getting annoying.

"This will give you one last chance to make sure you're choosing the right people! When the final round is over, we do one more tally and release the final results. Most people in the final round walk out with at least one match, sometimes all three! After that, we will work with you on a one-on-one basis to set up future dates with your matches. Any questions?"

"No!" Everyone said at once.

"Great! In your packet, there's a number. Dig that out and stand behind the chair with the corresponding number marked. You have one minute!" A bell rang out and people scrambled to find their spaces.

I stood between two women, one tall and one short. Neither of them acknowledged my presence. Fletcher was all the way at the end of the table behind me. She gave me a little wave before turning to face her match. The man in front of me wore glasses and had a crooked nose. He was a few inches taller than me and well-dressed.

"Hey, Toby," the shorter woman next to me said.

Toby, the man in front of me, blushed. "Hey, Cathy."

What kind of dating pool was this anyway?

"Everyone ready!" Lucy called.

More cheers and whistles.

The bell rang. "Ready? Set! Match!"

Chairs scraped from their places as everyone sat down.

Here we go...

EIGHTEEN

"Do you two know each other?" I asked.

"We do," Cathy said. "*Quite* intimately."

Aaagh. "Is that right?"

Toby had the grace to blush like a ripe tomato. "Cathy," he admonished.

"Oh, Toby." Cathy giggled. "You know you had fun."

Toby sighed.

I interrupted the trip down memory lane. "We only have four minutes. Ready to start?"

Toby nodded adamantly.

"I'm Addie."

"Toby."

"Are you a cat or dog person?"

"Dog."

Toby's turn. "Are you allergic to anything?"

Weird question, but okay. "Not that I'm aware of." I eyed him. "How many of these women have you dated?"

Toby blinked. His mouth opened, then shut, opened, then shut again. "Errr."

"Right," I said faintly.

The taller woman next to me was whispering to the man across from her. "Did you hear what happened to poor Aaron?"

Toby spoke again. "Is this your first time?"

"Yes." I strained to hear the conversation next to me.

"It's a shame," her potential match whispered back. "He'd been in the game for a while now."

The game. What game? A woman next to him hissed for him to shut up. He glared at her and returned his attention to his match. "Can you believe it? You think that girl did it? Harmony or whatever her name was?"

The woman snorted. "Harper? Hardly. She's a little mouse every time she comes here. I highly doubt she put two bullets in him."

Two bullets. How did she know he was shot? The autopsy report wasn't out yet. Our state made those reports public record, but Sean didn't even have the report yet.

"Do you have any kids?" I asked Toby.

"Nope."

This entire thing felt like death by a thousand paper cuts.

As if by magic, Lucy appeared and placed a hand on the woman's shoulder. "*Sienna.* How's it going over here?" Her red fingernails sank into Sienna's shirt.

The woman winced and swallowed hard. "Oh. Fine! Just getting to know my match."

I glanced at her. It sounded like she'd known the guy beforehand.

"Wonderful!" Lucy gushed. "Meeting someone for the first time can be *so* awkward."

The man across from her decided his napkin was the most interesting thing in the room. One thing was certain. Lucy ruled this thing with an iron fist. I needed to get closer to her to figure out what was going on.

The bell rang just as I was about to speak.

"Time to switch!" Lucy said through the mic, her chipper voice booming through the restaurant.

I dutifully got up and went to the next chair. This time it was a man named Hal.

"Hi," I said.

"Hello…" he squinted and leaned forward. "Addie?"

"Mmm hmm."

"Right." Hal adjusted his massive glasses and gave me a wobbly smile. Sweat beaded on his shiny forehead. "How are you tonight?"

"I'm dandy." I wish I would have listened to Hardy and stayed home. The only danger I was in was of drowning in cheap cologne and awkward small talk.

"Good, good," Hal said, his voice trailing off until we stared at each other.

I leaned in and went for gold. "Did you hear there was a murder?"

Hal blinked and narrowed his eyes. "I did."

"Did you know him?"

"Not really."

"Oh." I sat back and crossed my arms over my chest. "Things like that never happen in this town, so I was curious, that's all."

Hal shrugged. "I can't tell you much. Aaron got a lot more dates than I ever did."

Empathy squeezed me. "I'm sorry to hear that."

Hal waved the words away. "That's alright. It just means I haven't found the right person yet."

That...that was surprisingly sage. I tilted my head and studied him. He wasn't handsome exactly. Hal was overall plain, but he had bright cheery eyes and a friendly face. "Have you ever been married?"

"Once." A sad smile crossed his face. "I'm a widower."

"Oh. Goodness. I'm so sorry to hear that."

"It was a long time ago. I feel like I'm finally ready to get back out there."

"Have you been speed-dating long?"

Hal shook his head. "No. A friend of mine introduced me to this thing. I'm only a few months in. This is my second event."

"Well, I'm sure you'll do just fine." I offered a smile. It just wouldn't be with me.

"I see." Hal leaned back and studied me, a keen intelligence in his eyes I hadn't noticed when I first sat down.

"Are you local?"

I looked around the room, feigning confusion. "I think we're all local, aren't we?"

Hal paused for a long moment. "Sure. Yeah. I guess we are, aren't we?"

"Odd question, Hal." My laugh was a little bit too high-pitched.

"Was it?"

The bell rang. "TIME!"

Thank goodness. I smiled politely and rose, stepping over to the next chair. Hal's eyes lingered on me for a moment longer before he sat down.

Something was up with that guy. I didn't get murderer vibes off him, but there was more to Hal than met the eye.

Fletcher and I went through the exhaustive process for an hour and a half before the final bell rang.

I sank into my seat and closed my eyes while everyone else rose and headed straight for the bar.

Someone pressed a drink in my hand. I cracked an eye open and stared at Fletcher.

"Was that as painful for you as it was for me?" she asked.

"I'd like to drown myself in a tub of lukewarm bath water."

Fletcher snickered. "Courtesy of our friendly bartender. He saw me coming and had them ready for us before I got there."

I took a long sip and let out a sigh. "Is this how dating really is now?"

"Unfortunately." She shook her head. "Lots of men don't know how to talk to women anymore." Her lips twisted with amusement. "Not that they were ever great at it, but now they get all weird and sweaty and ask stupid questions like what's the length of my inseam."

I choked on my drink.

"Did you find anything interesting?" she asked, when I'd composed myself.

I leaned over and murmured my thoughts about Hal. No one was around us, but this place gave off a weird vibe. Listening devices under the table wouldn't surprise me.

"Interesting." Fletcher's eyes narrowed. "I heard a couple of people talking about him, but it sounded more gossipy than anything." She held up her card and waved it around. "But I added them to my card so I could press them later."

We high-fived. "Awesome. You're definitely going to get more matches than I am, but I checked Hal. He may check me just to press me for info."

"You think he's the guy?"

"No, but there's something about him I can't put my finger on."

"That guy with the weird glasses?" she asked.

"Yup."

"Huh." Fletcher looked away before he could feel her eyes on him. "He's kinda cute."

I blinked in surprise. "Are you serious?"

"Deadly. I think his glasses might be fake. Maybe he's in law enforcement."

I turned to look at him. Now that he was standing up, I could see what Fletcher was saying. His poorly fitted clothing didn't hide that he was in shape. "Hmm. Maybe." I got out of my phone and texted Hardy.

"Let's hope he matches you. Otherwise, this night might have been a colossal waste of time."

"You going on any second dates with anyone?"

Fletcher snorted. "Not a chance. But if Hal had been at my table, I'd consider it."

I shook my head at her and took another sip.

This night couldn't be over fast enough.

NINETEEN

Fletcher ended up with three matches, all the ones she'd selected.

I ended up with Hal.

We sat across from each other at a solo table, waiting for the other one to break first.

I was feeling a little bored and a lot feisty, so I decided to break the ice.

"Are you a cop?"

He reeled back like I'd slapped him, then leaned forward, teeth bared. "Are you out of your mind?" he hissed.

I grinned. "You didn't answer the question."

Hal glared at me. To anyone looking at us, they'd think this one-on-one date was getting off to a very wrong start. "Who are you anyway?"

"Addie Parker."

He rolled his eyes. "My left foot."

"Tell me if you're a cop, and I'll tell you who I am."

His nostrils flared. "You are insufferable."

"I've heard worse."

Hal's lips twitched. "Fine. What if I am?"

"You still didn't answer my question. What if you are?"

He stared at me for a beat before he muttered an unflattering curse. "You know I can find out whatever I want about you as soon as this is over, right?"

I lifted a shoulder in a careless shrug. "You can try."

He tapped his fingers on the table. "You're not here for a date at all, are you?"

"Nice try. I'm not telling you anything until you tell me who you are."

He blew out a breath. "Fine," he growled.

I held up a finger. "I'm going to confirm everything you say, so you better tell me the truth."

His eyes glittered with suppressed anger. "Quinn Bryant. FBI."

My eyebrows hitched. "Interesting." I typed the info into a text message and sent it to Hardy.

He sent back a brusque text. *Hold on.*

"And you?" Quinn asked.

I held up a finger and waited for Hardy to respond.

"Ladies and gentleman," Lucy's voice chirped, a hint of annoyance in her cheery tone, "it's rude to be on your phone during a date, so please be sure to stow all cellular devices."

Quinn smirked at me.

He's legit. If they're involved, you need to get out of there.

I put my phone away and leaned closer. "My name is Dakota Adair. I'm a private investigator."

"And who was on the phone?"

"My fiancé, former Detective Hardy Cavanaugh."

His expression cleared. "You're investigating the murder?"

I nodded. "You?"

He nodded. "And the woman who supposedly committed it."

"I don't understand why your agency is involved."

"Because this isn't the first death surrounding this company. It's been the subject of multiple BBB complaints, but not a single case has gone to court. They either have a fantastic lawyer, or they're bribing people to keep their mouth shut." Quinn's gaze flicked up. "Quick. Pretend you like me."

I put my chin on a hand and batted my eyelashes at him. "You are *so* funny," I said and giggled.

Lucy loomed over our table a second later. "You look like you two finally straightened out whatever it was bothering you." She smiled, but her voice was laced with suspicion.

Quinn reached over and took my hand, squeezing my fingers in warning when I tried to take it back. "Just a miscommunication. Right, Addie?"

My fake smile was worthy of a pageant. "That's right!

Hal is the *best!*" I gushed, squeezing the life out of his fingers.

"Well," Lucy said, looking a little nonplussed, "I'll let you two get back to it then."

She turned, and Quinn let go of my fingers like he was holding a poisonous snake. We waited for her to walk away before we spoke again.

"My friend and employee is accused of his murder. There's no way she did it. I'm here trying to find the truth."

"I don't think she did either," Quinn admitted. "But you need to stay out of my way. If you interfere in my investigation..."

I rolled my eyes. This was Hardy déjà vu all over again. "I'm being paid to run my own investigation. The best thing we can do is agree to work together."

Quinn snorted. "Unlikely."

I huffed an annoyed breath. "Are all law enforcement people as crabby as you are?" Hardy had been similar when he found me sniffing around his cases.

"I'm not crabby," Quinn pronounced. "I just won't have an unqualified investigator screwing up my hard work."

I gasped in outrage. "Unqualified! I'm licensed and have several cases under my belt!"

He chuckled, the sound so derisive it made me want to smack him. "Sure, honey."

"Oooh, that's it," I snapped. "You see that stunning redhead over there?"

Quinn's eyes flicked toward Fletcher. "What about her?"

"She thought you were cute and hoped to get a date."

His jaw dropped. Surprise and confusion flashed over his face, but I didn't give him the chance to respond.

I smiled evilly and held up my cell. "Fat chance now."

He lunged for my phone, but I whipped it out of the way before he could grab it. Hal spluttered as I quickly typed a text to Fletcher.

He's the worst. Run.

He looks madder than a wet hen, Fletcher replied. *Glad to see you still got it.*

I laughed.

"That was uncalled for," Quinn hissed.

"But very fun," I said, smiling sweetly at him. "Besides, you're sitting here with me, aren't you? Totally smitten."

"I'd rather gnaw off my own arm and deep fry it before going on a date with you."

"Ditto," I snapped.

We glared across the table at each other.

Quinn sighed. "We have to walk out of here together to keep the ruse up."

"If you touch me, you'll be missing an important appendage."

"Like I said, lady. I'd rather get bitten by a viper."

"You will if you keep being a jerk," I muttered.

The bell rang. "TIME!" Lucy called again. "We have time for one more round if you're still undecided. Just drop your selection card in the jar. Buuuuuuut," she drawled, "if you're happy with who you've chosen, and they're happy with you, make sure you switch phone numbers and let us know on the way out! We'll plan the best second date everrrrrr!"

"She is insufferable," Quinn said.

"Finally, something we can agree on."

I shot Hardy a text, letting him know I was walking out with the detective. We rose and walked over to Lucy, both of us wearing fake smiles.

"Oh good! You two hit it off. Wonderful!" She eyed us both. "Did you switch numbers?"

Not on your life. I nodded.

"Great! I'll make a note and get in contact with you both in a few days. Sound good?"

"Perfect," I said through gritted teeth.

"Can't wait," Quinn said, sounding like he'd rather drive his car right into the ocean.

Lucy gave us an odd look. "You know, it's so interesting to see the final couples. Even after all these years, I'm still surprised by some of the matches."

Quinn snagged me around the waist and pulled me closer, his grip like iron. "Opposites attract, you know?"

"Oh, I know," Lucy said with a wink. "Have a good evening, you two! And don't get too far ahead of yourselves before your second date, if you know what I mean!"

I'd rather stand motionless on a bed of hot coals.

Quinn let out a lascivious chuckle. "We'll try our best."

He turned and led us out. Fletcher's brows hitched up as I passed her.

"Don't wait up," Quinn said with a wink.

Fletcher burst out laughing. "Give me five, and I'll meet you in the car."

Quinn didn't give me time to respond.

When we made it outside, I tried to loosen his grip, but he held on tighter. "There are cameras out here," he hissed. "Try to pretend like my touch doesn't make your skin crawl."

I relaxed but lowered my head and barely moved my mouth when I spoke next. "If I had a knife, I'd stab you right in the heart."

"I don't have one, doll. Where you parked?"

"Toward the right. Dark sedan."

When we reached the vehicle, Quinn at least had the decency to open the door for me. Then he opened the back passenger seat and slid in.

Hardy bristled with rage. "Can I help you, Agent?"

"Yes. You can keep your nose out of my case."

Hardy's jaw tightened. "You can keep your hands off my fiancée, but I can't stay out of your case."

"You were telling the truth about having a fiancé?" His eyes darted back and forth between us.

"Yes," I said calmly. "I don't want to punch Hardy repeatedly in the face, so there's that."

Hardy's brows lifted, amusement shining in the depths of his blue eyes. "I take it you two hit it off?"

"Quinn is a bully," I pronounced.

Quinn snarled. "And you are the most aggravating, irritating—"

Hardy cleared his throat.

Quinn blew out a frustrated breath and lifted a hand. "My apologies. I'm investigating Speed Dating for Love for several violations of the law, but the murder takes precedence. I'm here to caution you about stepping on the agency's toes."

"I'm well aware of how to conduct myself during an investigation," Hardy said dryly.

Quinn pointed a finger at me. "It's her I'm worried about. She's not prior law enforcement."

"I didn't tell you that," I protested.

Quinn rolled his eyes. "You didn't have to. We're going to be stuck together for a while, thanks to the match we made."

Hardy glanced at me. "Match?"

"Not even a little bit like that. She knew I was up to something, and I suspected she was too. We decided to figure it out by choosing each other." Quinn's eyes sparkled. "But I would like to add that Dakota here only had one match. Me."

I rolled my eyes. "Because I only *chose* one. You, you knuckle-dragging Neanderthal."

If someone selected a potential match, but they didn't select that person back, the one who didn't get picked was disqualified unless they received another match. It seemed like getting picked last for gym class, but I wasn't here to date, so what did I care?

I smiled sweetly at Quinn. "So what does that say about you?"

He gave me a poisonous look back, which made me laugh.

"Are you two done?" Hardy asked, an amused note in his voice.

"The agency is setting us up on a date. We'll have to go with it. I wanted to tell you that in person. I have no designs on your lady." He grimaced. "None whatsoever. Even if she really was in the pool, I don't like blondes."

"I'm not blonde," I growled. "You really are the worst, you know that?"

"I try, doll." Without another word, Quinn slid out of the car, giving us a finger wave as he strode away.

I exhaled a frustrated, quiet shriek. "That guy is the worst!"

Hardy chuckled and started the vehicle. "How about we get home?"

"Don't forget Fletcher."

Hardy groaned. "Already did."

A familiar redhead popped out of the restaurant. "There she is."

Fletcher slid into the car a moment later, grinning from ear to ear. "How'd it go with Hottie McHal?"

I turned and pointed at her. "You are never allowed to say that ever again in my presence."

Hardy grinned and pulled out of the parking lot.

Home. *Finally.*

TWENTY

Harper was on the floor snort laughing as I told her about last night's speed-dating debacle. Izzy was somewhere in the back with Hardy, going through the box of new children's books I'd just gotten in.

"And this man...Quinn?"

I nodded.

"He thinks I'm innocent?"

"He does."

Harper closed her eyes and let out a slow breath. "That's good, right?"

"Very good. Quinn is a jerk, but he gave me no indication that he's not fully invested in proving who was responsible." I wasn't looking forward to the "date" we had coming up, but at least I could attempt to pry some info out of him.

"I wish there was something I could do." She untangled a strand of orange lights. "There's nothing worse than sitting around while other people decide your fate."

I sat down on the floor and grabbed the other strand of lights. "When you were at the event where you met, did you feel like he went after you on purpose?"

Harper frowned. "What do you mean?"

I busied myself with a pesky knot right at the end of the plug. "Did you feel like your connection was natural, or did Aaron push you into a relationship? Was he overly flattering right up front?"

Harper shrugged. "He told me I was beautiful and wondered why I was still single. He said I was the prettiest thing he'd ever seen." A tear rolled down her cheek. "I was so stupid."

"No. Never. Men like him are pros at making someone feel wanted. They prey upon younger, single women and promise them the moon. This is not your fault." It was Aaron's, or Michael, or whatever his name was, and I was beginning to suspect one of the women he'd done this to before Harper had found him and made him pay for his actions. It was only a theory I had now, but it was worth looking into.

"Is there anything I can do to help?" Now that we had all the lights untangled, Harper unfolded herself from the floor and started to string them up and around the window. The blinking soft orange and cream-colored lights screamed autumn more than anything else in my shop.

"Keep trying to remember anything that might help us." I thought about it. "Maybe search through all his belongings and see if there's anything we should take a look at."

Harper brightened. "I can do that! I haven't had the chance to go through everything yet. To be honest, I was putting it off, but if it helps in any way, I'm happy to do it." She pressed the last strand onto the double-sided tape and stepped away. "That looks great!"

I eyed the display. There were still a few final touches to go, but Harper and Izzy had done a wonderful job. "Looks amazing. You might even take Jack down."

Harper grinned, the happiest I'd seen her in weeks. "Let's hope!" She looked at the time and gasped. "I better get out of here before things pick up."

My heart hurt for her. We'd come two hours early to make Harper feel more comfortable. Izzy was a naturally early riser on school days, so it wasn't a big deal for all of us to wake up early and head over. It helped that we'd stopped for coffee on the way. "You don't have to go."

Harper's eyes softened. "I appreciate you saying that, but it's for the best. Hopefully, it's only temporary, but if it's not, I don't want the store to suffer."

"I don't care what anyone says, Harper. You're innocent. We both know it. If the residents here can't see that, then I don't want them in my shop."

Tears welled in her eyes. "I—I appreciate that so much. I appreciate you. But I'm going to go. For now." She gave me a weak smile and bent to pick the rest of the decorations up off the floor. "I'll come back in a few days and finish things up."

Izzy and Hardy appeared around the corner. Izzy gasped when she saw the blinking lights. "It's sooooo cute!" she gushed.

Harper grinned. "Thank you! I couldn't have done it without your help."

An adorable dimple appeared in Izzy's cheek when she smiled. "You're welcome!" She ran over and hugged Harper around the waist. Harper bent down and encircled her, squeezing Izzy before she stepped away and picked up the box.

"Alright. I'm out of here, folks. If I find anything in Aaron's belongings, I'll give you a call."

Hardy leaned against one of the shelves and nodded. "We'll keep you posted."

"Thanks." Harper put the box underneath the register area and waved as she headed out the door.

"Is Auntie Harper sad?" Izzy asked.

I crouched down and opened my arms, gathering Izzy up. "A little," I admitted.

"Is she going to be okay?"

"I think so. Daddy and I are helping her with something. Once it's over, I hope she will be right as rain."

She buried her cold nose in the crook of my shoulder. "I don't like it when she's sad."

I gave her a little squeeze. "Me neither." Scooping her up, I hoisted her onto my hip and jerked my head to the door. "It's still early. I think we have time for pancakes before school. What do you think?"

Izzy gasped and looked at Hardy. "Can we, Daddy?"

Hardy laughed and pushed away from the shelf. "Sure can. As long as you give me twenty-five bites."

"Twenty-five!" Izzy exclaimed.

"That's right."

"Four," she bargained.

We headed out the door, Hardy and Izzy bickering back and forth about how much of her pancakes to give up.

THE CALL CAME LATER that evening when Hardy and I were curled up with Izzy watching Malcolm in the Middle.

"Is this Addie Parker?" a female voice said.

It took me a moment to remember my false identity. "Uh, yes. This is she."

"Hi! This is Maria Evinera. I'm with Speed Dating for Love. How are you this evening?"

"I'm great, Maria. How are you?"

"So good!" Apparently, a chipper attitude ran in the Speed Dating for Love family. "I'm calling to set up your second date with Hal Bryant. Are you so excited?"

"*So* excited," I gushed, rolling my eyes at Hardy.

His eyes crinkled in amusement as he leaned closer to listen. "Great! I have a choice of two premium events, and we always allow the female to choose."

Err. That sounded a little sexist, but okay.

"Would you prefer a trip to the zoo or a day trip to Nashville with a sightseeing tour?"

Spending that much time with Quinn sounded pretty

terrible. I'd prefer neither. "Which one?" I mouthed to Hardy, covering the mouthpiece.

"Zoo," he whispered.

Zoos were awful. He gestured for me to hurry up and answer. I gave him a dark look. "Uh, the zoo, I guess."

"Wonderful!" Maria rattled off the itinerary. We'd go to the zoo before lunch and out to dinner afterward. Then there was a comment card to fill out and another card to determine whether we wanted to continue seeing each other. "I'll send you over an e-mail with a detailed itinerary. As always, your dates are completely covered as part of our premium concierge service included in your membership!"

"Sounds good, Maria. Thanks for letting me know."

We disconnected, and I glared at Hardy. "The *zoo*?"

My look of outrage made him laugh. "Hear me out."

"Better be good," I grumbled.

"It's the best place for you to exchange information without anyone overhearing. If you're on a tour, you'll be surrounded by people. You may not have a chance to discuss anything."

I hated that he was right. "Ugghhhhh," I groaned.

Izzy, half asleep between us, patted my leg sleepily. "It's okay," she murmured before snuggling deeper into her dad.

Hardy chuckled and gathered her up, rising to tuck her into bed. I followed behind him and waited until he was finished before I bent over her bed and pressed a kiss onto her forehead. By then, she was out like a light.

We shut the door behind us and headed back to the couch. It was still too early to go to bed, but neither of us wanted to do anything else. My phone dinged, signaling a text message.

I reached over and grabbed it off the coffee table.

Found something. Got a moment to chat?

I called Harper back right away.

"Hi!"

"Hey, Harper. Whatcha got?"

"I'm not sure if it's something or not. I found a small notebook tucked into Aaron's sock drawer. The only thing in it is a list of possible initials with what look like addresses and numbers to the side."

I told Hardy what she said. "Can she drive it over? Or can we come get it?" An urgent note in his voice made my stomach flip.

"Is it that important?" I asked.

"It could be."

"Harper, is there any way you can drive it over to us? If not, we can come pick it up. Hardy thinks it might be important."

She snorted. "Hmm. Let me check my social calendar," she said dryly. "I can be there in fifteen."

"Sounds good. Be careful."

I sat up once we hung up. "You know something."

"I *might* know something. I'll have to see the notebook."

"What do you think it might be?"

"If we're very lucky, it's a list of his victims. The

numbers could be anything. Birthdates, account numbers, monetary amounts."

I thought about it. "Harper would have recognized birthdates. If it's account numbers, we should be able to track down all his victims, right?"

"That's my hope."

We settled in to wait for Harper.

An hour passed, and she still hadn't arrived. I was starting to get concerned. I dialed her number, but the phone went straight to voice-mail.

"Hardy? Should I be worried?"

Hardy's expression was grim. He stepped into the kitchen and made a call. I heard Harper's name and description of her vehicle. Hardy listened for several long seconds, said a terse *thank you*, and hung up.

I stood, wringing my hands.

"Grab your coat. The babysitter is on the way," he said. "Harper is in the hospital."

TWENTY-ONE

I flew into the lobby, Hardy close behind me. The nurse who sat at the registration desk eyed me warily. My voice shook when I told her Harper's name and asked where to find her. The nurse pointed.

"Just down the hall. She's in room 302."

I took off at a sprint.

Harper sat on the hospital bed, a butterfly bandage on her forehead and sporting two rapidly blackening eyes. Her left arm was in a sling, cradled against her chest. Horror filled me at the sight.

I rushed into the room and hurried to her bed. "You're okay," I breathed, relief pounding through my veins.

"I am. My car isn't," she said.

I looked at Hardy. "On it." He stepped outside the room.

"What happened?" I pulled up a chair and moved it closer to her bed. "I'm so glad you're alright."

Harper's eyes flashed with anger. "Someone ran me off the road. My vehicle hit a tree and stalled out."

I closed my eyes. This could have been so much worse.

"I was lucky I wasn't speeding."

"They were looking for the book." I took her hand. "If I had known it was that dangerous, I never would have asked you to bring it to us."

"They were," she agreed. "The other vehicle stopped and the driver ran over to mine, but they weren't looking to make sure I was okay. My seatbelt had locked, and I couldn't get it undone. They searched the vehicle and took my purse." She grimaced. "Going to the DMV is *such* a pain."

This woman was lying here beat all to heck, and she was more concerned about the DMV. I had to laugh. That place *was* pretty awful.

The loss of the information was a big blow to our case, though. "That book must have been pretty important. It's a shame it's gone."

Harper grinned and dug into her bra, producing a small, flexible notebook. "Who said it was gone?"

I gasped. "Harper! You little genius!"

She shrugged, wincing with pain when she moved. "Ow. Ow. I had a feeling it was important when I looked deeper, so I thought, what's the safest place to stow something where normal people won't look?"

"The bra. Ever trusty holder for small things for as long as I can remember."

She held it out for me to take. "Keep it safe. This might be the only thing that helps us catch a killer."

I tucked it into my purse. "I'll give it to Hardy as soon as he gets back."

We chatted for a while about inane things. Harper was surprisingly alert for someone on serious pain meds. Hardy popped back into the room a while later. "Everything okay?" I asked.

"The vehicle is a total loss." Hardy winced in sympathy. "Unofficial until you get the final word from your insurance company, but it's impossible to drive."

Harper's face fell. She let out an *oh* of surprise and looked down at her hands, twisting in the sheets. "That's unfortunate. The other driver fled the scene, so there's no one to hold responsible."

"We'll find him," I swore. "I promise."

Harper nodded, her smile thin. "Would you mind asking when I'll be released?"

I stood, touching her knee as I rose. "I'll grab a nurse."

Hardy followed me outside.

"How bad is it?" I asked.

"Not great," he admitted. "That notebook must have a wealth of information someone doesn't want us to get our hands on."

"Oh!" I pulled the notepad from my purse.

Hardy's eyes widened before snatching it from my hand. He tucked it into his front pocket. "Harper should consider staying with us for a little while."

"I agree. She might not, but I'll suggest staying somewhere other than her house if she doesn't want to come home with us."

We flagged down a nurse and asked about Harper. The nurse told us she was being admitted for overnight observation because of the head wound. Harper was going to love that.

"I'll have a guard posted on her tonight," Hardy said.

I hugged his arm. "We're lucky to have you looking out for us."

"Come on. Let's go tell Harper so we can sit down and try to decipher this book."

HARPER WAS INDEED grumpy about staying in the hospital, but it helped that a handsome police officer showed up to guard her door. Her mood had brightened by the time we left. If there was ever a hint that Aaron was wrong for her, it would have been the pretty blush when the chiseled-jaw officer knocked on the door and introduced himself.

We relieved the babysitter when we made it home, paying her a little more than normal for the short notice and late call.

As soon as she was out of the house and we'd double-checked all the locks and window latches and peeked in on Izzy, Hardy and I retreated to the living room to see if we could decipher the notebook's contents.

Sitting beside him, I watched as he opened it and flipped through the pages. The scrawl was slanted to the right, spidery and hard to read. The left column had initials, the middle had addresses, and the right contained a list of numbers in no certain order. Some of them had eight numbers, while others had nine and even ten. On the end of those numbers were two letters—state abbreviations.

Hardy frowned, his eyes skimming through the pages.

"What is it?"

Hardy closed the book and didn't respond for a moment. "I think it's a list of victims, addresses, and their bank account numbers."

I sucked in a breath. "But that book is full."

"It is." He let out a long sigh. "This case has gotten much larger than us, I think."

"What are you going to do?"

He leaned back and crossed his arms behind his head, allowing me to snuggle into his chest. Hardy dropped an arm and toyed with my hair. "If this notebook belongs only to Aaron, can you imagine how many other victims there are with all those other people that have memberships?"

"I saw at least four states," I murmured, breathing in his scent.

"This explains why the feds are involved."

I thought about my "date" with Quinn and groaned. "Should we call him?"

Hardy grunted. "I'm not going to ruin my evening by talking to him. We'll call him in the morning."

"He's going to want the notebook."

"He can have it," Hardy said. "As soon as we make a photocopy of it."

I grinned up at him. "I like the way you think, Cavanaugh."

TWENTY-TWO

I was on a date with an insufferable FBI agent, whom I'd rather kill than kiss. We glared at each other over lunch. Quinn had a spot of ketchup on the side of his chin, and I didn't tell him because he was a jerk, and I hoped he walked around with it all day. In fact, I was thinking about smearing mustard on his shirt just to make him a canvas of condiments.

"Why are you staring at me?" he snapped.

I lifted a shoulder in a slow shrug. "Just wondering how that face of yours doesn't send women screaming from the room in droves."

Quinn smirked. He darn well knew he wasn't ugly. When I first saw him, I thought he was plain. The more time I spent with him, the more I realized how wrong I was. "Try again."

I rolled my eyes. "What did you find out about the notebook?"

"That's on a need-to-know basis, and you have no need to know." He took another bite of his hot dog. A dot of ketchup plopped onto his shirt.

Ha. It wasn't mustard, but it would do.

Quinn swore and dabbed at the stain but succeeded only in smearing it. I still didn't tell him about the smear on his chin.

"We didn't have to tell you about the notebook," I said.

His gaze flicked up to me. "Sure. If you want to add concealing evidence to your list of crimes."

"Crimes?" My eyebrows rose. "I think not," I said haughtily. Quinn really was the *worst*. "Your agency already went through his belongings, didn't you? So, someone thought it was unimportant. There's no concealing of anything, and remember, we didn't have to tell you about this. We've done what we were supposed to, but you've failed to keep us in the loop about anything concerning the case."

Instead of being chastised, Quinn rolled his eyes. "I don't have to share a thing with you. In fact, anything I tell you has the potential to jeopardize the case. While I appreciate your telling me about the notebook, I'm afraid I can't reciprocate in kind."

"Is that so?" I murmured, studying him. I plopped my chin on my hands and batted my eyes. "Tell me, Quinn. Are all agents as completely insufferable as you are?"

Quinn snorted and took another bite of his hotdog. "I'm afraid so."

"Good to know." The burger before me had gone cold,

and I pushed it away, my appetite lost. "I'm afraid we're at an impasse then. Any information sharing on our part is over."

Quinn stared at me for a long moment before shrugging. "Alright then."

"Can we call this over now?" I waved my hand at the lunch and zoo.

He smirked. "I'm afraid not. We're stuck together until after dinner."

"Can we not and just say we did?" I whined.

"As much as I wish we could, I've come to realize these people closely watch their members. If we don't go, it will rouse suspicion. Since we're both there under false pretenses, it won't go well for either of us."

"Can't we tell them we're incompatible?"

"We have to finish the date first," Quinn said. He scarfed down the rest of his hot dog and eyed my burger. "Gonna eat that?"

I shook my head and pushed it over to him feeling slightly queasy.

Quinn reached for it and took a huge bite.

"Gross," I muttered.

Quinn's hearty laugh made me smile. Just a little.

Several hours later, we were beat. I decided I liked Quinn a little better when he was tired. He didn't talk as much, and when he did speak, it was to spout off interesting facts. I'd never met a man who knew as much about sloths as he did. It was weird and kind of hilarious.

. . .

"HAVE YOU EVER MET HARPER?" I asked him as we walked out of the zoo. Quinn carried a stuffed sloth and a balloon that said, "Sloths 4 Life!" He won it after knocking down six sloth bowling pins in a row at the game area set up toward the back area behind the snake exhibit.

"No. My partner interviewed her, but I've never spoken to her."

"Do you think you should?"

I thought they might hit it off. As much as I would like to pretend I'd never met Quinn, for now I was stuck with him. While I found him insufferable, he possessed a boyish enthusiasm about life I thought might appeal to my friend. Not that they could date now. She was a murder suspect, which would turn even the most stalwart of single men away. But once we cleared her name, the world might be her oyster.

For all his faults, Quinn was handsome and intelligent, and Harper could do a lot worse than him.

"I trust my partner's interview was thorough." We walked to our vehicles. "Meet you at the restaurant?"

I nodded. "See you there."

When I got into the vehicle, I let out a long sigh and thumped my head against the backrest a few times before I called Hardy.

He answered on the first ring. "Everything okay?"

"Besides Quinn being the worst? Yes."

Hardy's rumbling laugh made me smile. "As much as I know you don't want to hear this, I'm very glad you can't stand him."

"I only have room for one moody law enforcement officer in my life," I said, though I softened the words with a smile.

"Good. Are you heading out to dinner next?"

"Yes," I grumbled. Before I left, I'd given him a copy of our itinerary.

"Since the place is paying for it, I'd get the lobster."

"Definitely. I'm feeling the surf and turf and a couple of martinis."

My fingers tightened around the phone when Hardy chuckled. I missed him. "I should be home no later than 9:30."

"Good."

We chatted for a little while before I brought up the other reason I called him. "Quinn refuses to share info. I told him the notebook tip would be the last one we gave him."

"I'm not surprised. Government entities are always hesitant to share information, even with other agencies."

"He threatened me with concealing evidence charges."

"I wish he would try," Hardy snarled.

A soft and fuzzy feeling settled into my stomach. "Regardless, Quinn won't be an ally to us like we thought he might. Did you find anything out about the numbers?"

"Definitely bank accounts. I think we should take the time to visit a couple of the women on this list in the next couple of days. There are at least a few not too far away from here."

I'd have to call the other employees to see if they could

fill in for me. Fortunately for me, they were usually amenable to snapping up extra hours. "That should be doable."

"At least get a good meal out of tonight."

"I will. We have to fill out a card after dinner telling the place whether we still want to continue to date. Since Quinn has no intention of helping us, I don't see the point in continuing the charade."

"I'm happy to hear you say that. Hurry up and come home to me, Dakota."

"Always." We hung up, and I pulled out of the parking lot to attend one more painful event with Quinn Bryant.

TWENTY-THREE

Quinn and I barely spoke throughout the meal. I focused on the food and was pleasantly surprised by the offerings. Quinn's eyebrows rose when I ordered.

"I guess you're hungry," he mused.

"I'm not going to pass up a free meal. Plus, I ordered enough to take some back home."

"To your fiancé."

"Yup. What about you?" I realized I hadn't asked him about any significant others. He told me he was widowed, but that was before I'd pegged him as an agent. He might have lied about his past to make me feel more at ease. "Anyone waiting at home for you?"

His eyes flickered with grief before he schooled his expression.

"Oh," I said quietly. "You were telling the truth."

"I'll never lie about my wife," he said simply.

"I'm sorry. It's apparent you loved her very much."

Some of my dislike faded away. Holding a grudge against a man who was obviously deeply in love with his wife wasn't as easy as I expected. "Would you tell me something about her?"

His expression softened. "She was beautiful and smart. And much wiser than me."

My heart ached for him. "I'm so sorry for your loss."

Quinn grunted. "Me too."

I thought about what he was doing and how much it probably bothered him to go through this charade. "How did you end up with this assignment?"

A thin smile crossed his lips. "We figured out the speed-dating company was a likely front for fraud. My partner is married with several kids. His wife was not on board with him going on multiple dates with strange women."

"And you got volunteered?"

"More like volun*told*." He spread his hands out. "So here I am. Back in the dating pool."

"It could be worse," I volunteered.

One of his eyebrows rose. "Oh?"

"Yeah. I could actually like you."

He burst into genuine laughter. "True. I don't think we have anything to worry about, so perhaps this was lucky on both of our parts." Quinn picked up his drink and took a sip. "Speaking of, I have a...request." He winced. "More like a favor to ask."

I sat back in my chair and studied him. "A favor?

When you won't help us out at all while I'm trying to clear my friend's name?"

"It's different," he growled. "This has nothing to do with the investigation. It's...personal."

"Color me intrigued." I motioned for him to go on.

Quinn shifted uncomfortably. "We have those cards we have to fill out when this is over."

"Yes," I agreed. "I will derive great pleasure from checking *no* when I get to the question about going out with you again."

Quinn's jaw clenched. "What would you say to checking *yes*?"

I blinked in surprise. "Why would I do that?" I asked slowly.

He toyed with his napkin nervously. "Because you know who and what I am. I don't have to make inane small talk or fake interest, and honestly, pretending I want a relationship is the worst part of this assignment."

I studied him for a long moment. Asking for this bothered him. *Really* bothered him. "What's in it for me?"

Quinn huffed a laugh. "My goodwill?"

I snorted. "We both know how much I care about that. You'll have to do better."

Quinn pushed his food away. "I have to admire your bloodthirstiness. I'm asking because I'm a widower, and you're trying to turn my pain to your advantage."

My jaw dropped. Of all the nerve. "And you're manipulating me by trying to make me feel guilty over asking for something in return because you know I owe you nothing and that you've been a jerk from the second we met!" Seriously. What was with this guy?

Quinn and I glared daggers at each other from opposite sides of the table.

"Fine," he snapped. "What do you want?"

"Information."

"No."

I pulled the card from my purse and clicked the pen, hovering it over the word *no*.

"Wait." Quinn snatched the pen from me.

"I'll check it in blood if I have to."

He sighed and shook his head. "Please, Dakota."

A laugh cracked from me. "You are seriously the most manipulative man I've ever met."

Quinn's jaw clenched so hard I could practically hear his teeth grind. "I can't give you info."

"Can't or won't?"

"Can't," he emphasized. "I'd jeopardize my job."

"If we told," I pressed.

His chest rose with the deep breath he pulled in. Quinn rubbed his chin. "We barely know each other. Why should I trust you?"

I opened up a little. "My fiancé is former law enforcement, and I'm a P.I. who runs a bookstore. He has an adorable little girl whose mother abandoned her. I love them both very much. Harper is a good friend of mine who also happens to be a valued employee. There's no way she did this. All I want to do is clear her name. I don't care about this dating agency. You can have all the glory, or whatever it is you're looking for when you bust them. I only want Harper's freedom."

Quinn studied me. "You could be lying."

"Just like you've been lying to me since the second I met you?"

His lips twisted. "It's not the same."

"Sure. Tell me all about how lying is okay for you but not okay for me because you're all important, and I'm just a peon P.I." I pressed my index finger between my brows, feeling the beginning of a headache coming on. "Why don't you come over for dinner tomorrow?"

Quinn jerked like I'd slapped him. "What? Why would I do that?"

"To get to know us, dummy." This freaking guy. "I'll cook. You hang out with Hardy. We'll talk. If I like you a little better tomorrow, I'll go along with this insanity. If Hardy agrees. And if you agree to share information with us. You're asking for a lot and offering nothing in return. I have zero interest in getting involved in your case. I'm only concerned for my friend."

The server came over with a dessert menu. Quinn shook his head, but I snatched the menu from his hand. "Uh. Speak for yourself. I'm definitely getting cake."

The server slowly backed away and promised he'd come back in a few minutes.

"With coffee, please!" I called.

"Two!" Quinn added. He shook his head. "You're a... lot."

I smiled. "Yup. I also want cake."

When the server returned, Quinn had somewhat thawed on his no dessert stance and ordered the creme brulee while I ordered Italian creme.

"Alright," he said when the server had left.

"Alright, what?"

"Dinner. I'll come."

"Good. I hope you like pasta. It's my specialty."

He dipped his head. "I do."

I motioned for him to hand me his phone. "Let me put our address in."

"I'll have a different car just in case someone is watching me."

"Makes no difference to us. Just let us know when you're a few minutes away."

The server returned with our desserts. When we finished and said our goodbyes, Quinn crossed his arms over his chest and leaned against his vehicle. "You really care about this woman?"

"Harper?"

He nodded.

"Of course I do. I've known her for years. She won't even dog-ear a page in a book. There's no way she killed that guy."

"For what it's worth, I believe you." Quinn opened the door and slid in. "I'll see you tomorrow, Addie."

Rolling my eyes, I waved and got into my car.

Now I just had to convince Hardy to give this bizarre situation a chance, and hope he didn't blow a gasket.

TWENTY-FOUR

To Hardy's credit, he admitted it was weird, but if it got us the info we needed to get Harper out of trouble, he'd go along with it. He softened up even more when I told him about Quinn's wife and why he was asking for something in return.

Hardy opened a bottle of wine and poured us both a glass, leaving the third empty until Quinn arrived.

He'd texted a few minutes ago, letting us know he was only five minutes out. The doorbell rang shortly after, and Quinn walked in holding a bottle of red wine.

He shook hands with Hardy, nodded to me, and smiled at Izzy, who was peeking out from behind her dad.

"Hello," Quinn said, crouching down to her height. "I'm Quinn."

"Izzy." She gave him a gap-toothed smile, making him laugh.

"It's very nice to meet you." Quinn rose and handed

the bottle to Hardy. "I'm afraid I can't cook, but I can bring the wine."

Hardy set it down next to the open bottle and poured Quinn a glass. Izzy stayed glued to Hardy's side the entire time until the doorbell rang again a few minutes later.

"Auntie Harper is here!" I called, tapping the wooden spoon on the edge of the pot before I set it down and hurried to answer the door.

Izzy squealed with excitement.

After Harper got out of the hospital, she decided to stay with her parents instead of us. When we told her about Quinn, she offered to pick Izzy up and take her to the movies. Harper stepped in and scooped the wriggling kid up, giving her a tight hug.

"Ready to go see Beetlejuice?" she asked.

Izzy nodded. "Can I get popcorn?"

"If your dad says it's okay." Harper's smile faded when she noticed Quinn. "Hello."

Quinn looked like he'd seen a ghost. "Uh. Hello." He stood and extended a hand, staring at Harper intently. "Quinn."

"Harper. Nice to meet you."

"Likewise."

The conversation died, but they just kept staring at each other. My eyebrows lifted, and I looked at Hardy, who stared at them with a bemused expression.

I cleared my throat, snapping them out of whatever this was, and dropped a kiss on Izzy's cheek. "Thanks so much for taking her out for a little while. I'll save some pasta for you."

"No need," Harper assured me. "Mom has been cooking like we're having a hurricane party. The fridge is bursting with food. Thank you, though."

"You're staying with your parents?" Quinn asked.

"I am." The edges of her eyes tightened. "After the accident, staying by myself didn't seem wise."

Quinn stiffened. "Accident?"

Harper's brows drew together. "Yes. Someone ran me off the road to get that notebook."

Anger flashed in Quinn's eyes. "I see. Did you call the police?"

Harper stared at him. "Of course I did."

"I wasn't notified."

Harper's lips twisted to the side. "Well, Agent Quinn, I'm afraid I don't have your direct line, do I?"

"I can give it to you," he said.

I pressed my lips together. What was happening right now?

"Were you harmed?" Quinn pressed. "Your arm. Is that due to the accident?"

She still wore a cast, but she'd switched it from the bone-white color to a screaming hot pink.

"I spent the night in the hospital, but other than this, some sore ribs, and a bump on the head, I'm fine."

Quinn's face went blank. "I wouldn't call that *fine*." He pulled out his phone and sent a text. "I've requested a car at your house."

Harper snorted and held up a hand. "Totally unnecessary. I'm not there right now. My parents have a gated house and good security."

"I insist."

She straightened and bristled, anger sparkling in her bright eyes. "And I'm sure it's not necessary."

"And I insist," Quinn repeated. "It's done. Someone will be there tonight."

Harper huffed, not taking her eyes off Quinn, and grabbed the bag of Izzy's stuff I held out. "Some coloring books and markers, just in case."

"Thank you." She finally looked away from Quinn. "I'll have her back by 10."

I booped Izzy's nose. She wrinkled it and laughed. "Have fun, you two." I reached out and hugged Harper. "Be careful."

"Mom and Dad are in the car. They're coming with us." I loved Harper's parents. They came into the bookstore on occasion and bought a book or two—anything Harper recommended, they picked up. Married for over thirty years, they were adorable together, and loved Harper like crazy.

"Good." Izzy had my mom and Gran, but having another set of wonderful parents to spend time with might be good for her.

Hardy hugged Izzy and nodded at Harper. "Call us if you need anything."

"I will." Harper waved, her gaze lingering on Quinn before she and Izzy walked out the door.

"Well," I said, and clapped my hands, completely ignoring the weird vibe between him and my friend. "Dinner will be ready in about twenty minutes. How about we chat for a while?"

I could cut the tension in the air with a knife, and I'd *definitely* be pressing Harper about it later. But for now, Hardy and I needed to get Quinn to trust us.

IT WENT WELL, as odd dinners went. Hardy and Quinn had more in common than they wanted to admit. When one of them would bring up a topic the other was interested in, I'd notice their eyes light up before they remembered who the other one was, and they'd suddenly feign disinterest. I wanted to knock both of their heads together. This entire thing would be much easier if we all got along.

Though I could see Hardy's side.

It was weird to be friends with the man who wanted to continue fake-dating your fiancée.

What I also noticed was Quinn kept shifting the conversation back to Harper and trying to fish information out of us. Quinn was interested in her, but I didn't dare tease him for fear he'd shut down and Harper would suffer.

Quinn didn't seem to be the kind of man who would punish her, but if I was right and he was interested in her in a romantic way, I wouldn't jeopardize it for either of them. They both had a lot of baggage to work out.

The potential murder charges were also a massive complication.

I stayed mostly mum about Harper. If he wanted more information about her, he'd have to ask her.

By the end of the evening, Quinn had grown on me a little bit, and even Hardy was coming around. My fiancé needed more male friends in his life. He always kept a wall up between him and the other police officers because he had a lot of responsibility and didn't want the lines blurred. But Hardy was no longer a police officer, and Quinn didn't work in the same agency or department.

The only thing that might damage a budding friendship between them was them. And me, if I decided I couldn't stand seeing Quinn's face when all the chips finished falling, and that would depend on whether Harper was a free woman and completely cleared of all wrongdoing.

A lot of *ifs* there.

When dinner was over and I'd taken the plates to the kitchen, Quinn and Hardy got into a quiet discussion, their heads close and expressions intense. I turned on the water to avoid overhearing them and rinsed everything off. When I turned around, things seemed calmer somehow.

"Dakota?" Hardy called.

I came over and sat beside him. "Everything good?"

"I agree," Quinn said.

Just because it was Quinn, I decided to be difficult. "Oh? Agree to what?"

Quinn rolled his eyes. "Do we really have to do this again?"

"Depends." I smiled at him.

Hardy gently elbowed me.

"Alright," Quinn said. "I'm sorry for being a difficult, crotchety old man."

My eyebrows rose.

"And I'm sorry for not trusting you. But—"

"And you were doing so well," I said with a sigh.

"Buuuuut," Quinn continued, "my job makes me naturally suspicious of everyone, and you're defending a woman who's accused of murder."

"That you don't think she committed either!"

Quinn held his hands out and laughed. "I'm trying to apologize."

"You could have fooled me!" I snapped.

Hardy burst out laughing. "You two are like fire and gasoline."

I pinched the space between my brows. "I'm sorry. I'm being difficult just because I can. Alright. I check *yes*. We continue to go on painful outings, and we share information about Harper?"

Quinn nodded. Hardy sat back and studied us, a contemplative expression on his face. "What if," he began, then paused and rubbed his chin.

We stared at him expectantly.

"What if we double-dated?"

Quinn frowned. "Double-date? With whom?"

Hardy, you clever little devil, I thought. I knew exactly

what he was doing. "That's a great idea!" I breathed. "Are you thinking of the same person I am?"

"Harper?" Hardy asked.

Quinn's cheeks colored. I pretended not to notice. "Yes! You and Harper can come, and we can chat about this case together without looking suspicious!"

"I don't know about that," Quinn began.

"We can make sure it's not against the rules," I said. "It might not be a good idea to be out and about with Harper much, but we can always plan things outside the city limits. The zoo isn't close, and that's where they sent us last time, so it might work."

"Harper is a member. They won't want her dating someone who isn't on their speed dating roster."

I looked up at Hardy. "How do you feel about becoming a member?"

Hardy grinned. "I thought you'd never ask."

And so it was decided. To make this more comfortable for everyone, we decided to become a quartet. That way, Hardy was with us when I had to go out with Quinn, and Harper was with us to discuss the case. And...so those two crazy kids could get to know each other better. This could only benefit Harper. Even if there wasn't a romantic connection at the end, anyone who spent time with Harper would know she wasn't a killer.

And maybe, if things went really well, one day there would be a different kind of happy ending in store for those two.

TWENTY-FIVE

The days flew by as I scrambled to get everything set up for the next event. Books and Beaus got a rousing response from the community, though I had to be very careful about keeping my role secret. Instead, I made Harper the event's public face, though I sent all inquiries through Lucy.

Hardy had no trouble with his membership, and the lucky guy didn't even have to wear a disguise. Lucy hadn't noticed him at the club, and she welcomed him with annoyingly open arms.

"Have you found anything out about Lucy?" I asked Quinn as we filled the umpteenth balloon with helium.

"She's clean on paper. Nothing of concern in her background, either."

I only wished it could be that easy. If she had a long rap sheet, it might be a lot easier to figure out her reasoning. Instead, all we had was money. Granted, that was a good enough reason, but Lucy came from a good family and had money outside of the dating agency. What was her goal?

Derek was another one we hadn't figured out. He was obviously involved somehow, but we couldn't figure out the link between them.

We'd tailed him a few more times but only saw the blonde woman one more time. The last time he was with another woman, evidence we had yet to bring back to his long-suffering wife.

After tonight's event, Izzy was going to stay with Hardy's sister for the weekend, and Hardy and I were going to visit four people on the notebook's list. Quinn wasn't excited about the idea of us going without him, but his partner had dismissed the notion as useless. Strange, but Quinn said his partner was more interested in bringing Lucy down first. He didn't think Aaron's prior victims could help us more than his current ones.

Harper came in, struggling to carry a massive box. Quinn made a beeline for her the second he spotted her, leaving me alone with about two hundred more balloons to go. I glared at his back, but I wasn't angry. Quinn gravitated to Harper like he was a moon in her orbit, and Harper blushed every time she saw him.

It was teeth-achingly adorable.

But I still needed help with these blasted balloons.

Hardy spotted me and headed over. "Ditched again?"

"Yes," I said with a sigh. "I could be drowning in the river, and if he spotted Harper, he'd let me sink."

Hardy chuckled and took over the balloons, carefully placing them on the nozzle while I filled them.

"You up for one more night of surveillance before we go visit Mrs. Monroe?"

"After this?" I looked up in surprise. "It could be a late night."

"She called and gave us an address. Plus, she offered double our daily rate."

My eyebrows hitched up. Our daily rate wasn't exactly cheap. Doubling it meant we could dump all that money back in the business and not have to tap into our savings. Always the goal of a business, wasn't it? Being in the black?

"Alright. As long as you buy me coffee."

Hardy grinned. "I shall endeavor to buy you coffee for as long as my stalwart heart beats."

"No need to be dramatic," I said with a smile.

Quinn walked the heavy box over to the table and set it down, chatting with Harper as they walked outside and back to her car. She was responsible for the rest of the decorations and had apparently taken that duty to heart. The next time they walked in with a bigger box, then went out for one more.

"Can we bring Poppy with us this weekend?" She'd been a little absent with everything going on, as if she knew exactly how high the stakes were this time and felt the need to bury her head in the sand. She'd stayed with Izzy mostly and hadn't even come out to investigate Quinn when we'd had him over for dinner the other night.

"Of course. We'll need to book a pet-friendly place, but that's not a big deal."

"Thanks. If she doesn't want to come, I'll leave her, but it feels like she's almost in a depression."

"Izzy is soaking up all the time with her, but I agree. She's normally a lot more active, and the poor thing is lying around all the time."

Worry coiled in my stomach for her. "Maybe we should bring her tonight, too."

Hardy glanced up at me. "You're really worried about her, aren't you?"

I shrugged. "She's not acting like herself. If things don't get better, I'll probably take her to the vet soon."

"Good call. If you really want her to come, I'll go pick her up before the event ends."

I sighed. "No. That's okay. I'm being a worrywart. Plus, this is your first event, and I have a feeling you'll be the belle of the ball."

Hardy grimaced. "Are you and Quinn participating?"

"Yep. It's apparently our last chance to be sure this is what we want before we're pulled off the roster and move onto stage two."

"Stage two?"

Quinn and Harper came over then. "Exclusive dating," he said with a grimace.

The look on his face made me laugh. "Yes, it's exactly as awful as it sounds."

"Nothing against you, Dakota. It's just going to be more difficult to talk to people."

"Maybe you should have rethought the whole 'let's keep dating' thing," I said.

He shrugged. "No. The actual speed-dating part of this thing is painful. I like knowing where I stand and knowing it won't go anywhere."

"I'm sure it helps that we can barely tolerate each other," I said dryly.

Quinn laughed. "You're growing on me, Adair, but I like your fiancé better."

"Yeah," I said deadpan. "Me too."

Harper pointed to the boxes. "Am I good to start setting up?"

"Yup. We're the only ones here. I'd say we have an hour before Lucy and the others arrive. Plenty of time, and once I finish with these awful balloons, I can help."

"I'm happy to assist with the decorations," Quinn said quickly.

"Or you can ask Quinn," I said to Harper.

Harper eyed him. "I'm very particular about decor," she said slowly. "If I show you how to do it, I want it to look exactly like I want it."

A smile tipped Quinn's lips. "Yes, ma'am. I aim to please."

They walked off with Harper gesturing animatedly.

"If only he were that agreeable with me," I grumbled.

Hardy snorted. "Focus on the balloons, woman. The faster we get out of here, the faster we can finalize the Morgan case and get paid."

"Aye aye, Captain," I said dryly.

In response, Hardy popped another balloon onto the tank.

TWENTY-SIX

Attendees started showing up an hour and a half later. I was already tired, and it hadn't even started yet. Now that Lucy and the others were here, Hardy was careful to keep his distance. The plan was he'd match with me and Harper, and no one else, unless he found someone he thought might know more about Aaron.

I didn't love that Hardy was doing the same thing I did and that I'd have to watch him going on "dates" with other women, but if he could swallow his pride for the job, then so could I. Reacting in any way, shape, or form might blow the case and all the hard work we'd put into it.

Not that the evidence supported all our work. We barely had anything—only a bunch of dangling pieces of evidence we couldn't figure out how to put together. Multiple suspects, no real alibis among them. We'd checked the restaurant interior where we had our engagement dinner and saw no cameras. They only had exterior cameras and a few in the dining room. Nothing in the kitchen or back areas where the employees were.

Lucy's voice rang throughout the room half an hour later, chipper and annoying as always. A few minutes later, we were situated in front of our respective dates.

This guy was clean-cut and pleasant-looking, but he wore a bored expression, and I could tell he'd rather be chatting with the pretty redhead next to me and not me.

I didn't let it hurt my feelings. There was nothing more that I wanted than to close the case and never hear the words "speed-dating" again for as long as I lived.

"Hello," I said pleasantly.

"S'up," the guy responded.

I barely held in my groan. Squaring my shoulders, I slapped a smile on my face.

The bell rang.

Here we go again...

HARDY LOOKED shell-shocked when we finally made it to each other. I had to stop myself from reaching across the table and taking his hand. Quinn, sitting beside Hardy, gave me a warning look. Barely restraining the urge to glare at him, I tucked my hands in my lap and kept them there.

"Hi," Hardy said, his rumbling baritone making my stomach flip.

"I bet your card is full. Find anything you like?"

A slow grin curved his lips. "Not until a moment ago."

Quinn snorted.

The bell rang again.

Quinn sat in front of me this time. We stared at each other.

"Hello, darling," I said.

Quinn's eyes danced with dark amusement.

"You look lovely this evening, Addie."

I pressed a hand to the buttons of my cardigan. "Oh? This old thing?"

We chatted inanely until the bell rang again.

And again.

And again.

Then, finally it was over.

I slumped against the wall with relief. Quinn came over a few minutes later. To avoid suspicion, Hardy went to the bar and ordered a drink. The gaggle of women who quickly surrounded him made me want to scream.

"You did well," Quinn said.

"This is painful," I admitted. "I think I'd rather climb into a lion's den and sit motionless while it made a meal out of me than ever do this again."

Quinn chuckled. "I hear you. Find anything interesting?"

I shook my head. "Part of me is beginning to wonder if this is a huge waste of time."

"This sort of investigation takes forever. I still can't tell who's hired by this place and who is an unwitting member." Quinn shook his head. "Regardless of all that, I'd like to thank you."

I glanced up at him. "Oh? For what?"

He glanced at Hardy who was currently fending off no less than a dozen women.

"Well, for sticking with me so I didn't have to go on multiple dates."

I shrugged. "You saved me, too, technically."

"Maybe, but you could have walked away and thrown me to the wolves, and you didn't do that."

I shrugged. "I got something out of it."

Quinn snorted. "I'm sure you could have gotten it anyway."

It was probably true, but I wouldn't admit it. "We're doing surveillance tonight. Want to come?"

He tilted his head, curiosity sparking in his eyes. "Who's the target?"

"A guy named Derek Morgan."

Quinn recognized the name from our prior talks. "More infidelity?"

"The wife says so. She's building a case against him and wants a little more evidence."

"This is the same guy you saw giving money to Lucy?"

I nodded.

"I'll come. Nothing better to do tonight."

I grinned up at him. "No ladies catching your eye?"

He grimaced. "This isn't my thing. Never will be."

"I hear you. If I ever have another case like this come across my desk again, I'm turning it down."

Quinn chuckled. "How did a bookstore owner become a private investigator?"

I settled against the wall and told the story, answering

Quinn's thoughtful questions when he asked. When I finished, he asked something unexpected.

"How did Harper fit into it?"

"The store or the P.I. business?"

"Does she work there or only at the bookstore?"

"Only the books part. She started off as an assistant and moved her way up. I recognized I couldn't do it without her, and compensated her accordingly."

Hardy came over then, stalling our conversation. He deliberately chose to stand by Quinn, but his eyes burned as he looked at me. "I marked two matches," he growled. "They know more than they're letting on."

Jealousy burned in my gut, but I squashed it down.

"Which ones?" Quinn asked.

While they compared notes, I watched Lucy. She flitted around the room, smiling and chatting. I pushed away from the wall and followed her when she headed to the bar.

"Hi!" I gushed, stepping up beside her to order a vodka tonic.

Her eyes flickered. "Hello...Addie?"

I nodded. "Thanks so much for letting me take on an event. It seems like it's going well."

She smiled thinly. "Yes, this place was a good call. It's the perfect size to handle everyone."

"I'd love to host another one soon!"

Lucy shook her head. "We won't be here too much longer."

My fingers tightened around the glass. "Oh? Not enough membership here?"

Lucy shook her head. "Our company travels. We've been here too long already. With what happened to poor Aaron, we can't afford to stick around for too much longer."

"Did they ever find who did it?" I asked.

Lucy shrugged. "Looks like an old girlfriend."

I put a hand on my chest. "You think she really did it?"

Lucy took the second glass and turned to face me. "Of course she did. She's the only one with enough of a motive." She started to walk away.

"When are you leaving?" I called.

"Within the week." Lucy didn't look back.

The event finally ended. Hardy extracted more information than either of us expected, including a tidbit about seeing Aaron meeting with one of the other members days before his death. Someone who wasn't Alice.

"I invited Quinn to hang out with us later."

Hardy's eyebrow quirked. "During surveillance?"

"I realize that's weird, but yes."

"Let's leave now. This place gives me the heebie-jeebies." He glanced at Quinn. "I'll text you the address. Wait ten minutes before you follow."

"See you soon," I said, not liking that I had to ride with Quinn and not my fiancé.

"I'll stop and get you coffee." He leaned forward, caught himself, and shook his head. "I can't wait until this case is over," he growled.

Quinn wiggled his fingers. "I'll bring your lady back to you in one piece."

Hardy shot him a dark look and stalked away.

"You shouldn't keep antagonizing him," I admonished.

"And take away the only joy in my life right now?"

I followed Quinn to the coat rack. He helped me into mine and led me out the door, stopping periodically to say goodbye.

Right before we left, Lucy stepped in front of us. "Hello, Hal." Her eyes glittered with anger.

"Lucy." Quinn closed his fingers over my elbow. "Thank you for a wonderful event. If you'll excuse us, Addie and I would like to grab a bite to eat."

She held up a perfectly manicured finger. "Hold on, please." Lucy consulted the clipboard she held, flipping a few pages before she clicked her tongue. "You've been with us for a few months now and never showed any interest in any of our members until Addie arrived."

Quinn shrugged. "What can I say? There's only one Addie."

"Mm hmm." Lucy tapped her finger on the first sheet the clipboard held. "Most of our members match with at least four people during their first month with us. We like for them to play the field." She glanced at me and sniffed. "I'm not saying Addie isn't adequate, but..."

Quinn's jaw tightened. "It appears that's exactly what you're saying. Why don't you cut the baloney and say what you really mean?"

I moved closer to Quinn.

Lucy's nostrils flared. "Who are you working for?"

Uh oh.

"Working for?" Quinn's confused look was so believable I almost forgot he was an agent.

"Yes," Lucy snapped. "Is it Divine Daters? Did they send you here to infiltrate?"

I almost sagged with relief.

"Or did Markie send you in as a spy?"

Markie. Why did that name sound so familiar?

"I have no idea what you're talking about. I was widowed a few years ago. This is the first time I've wanted to get back into the dating pool. Addie was the first person I wanted to go out with in a very long time. I'm paying you for the privilege of dating her, but I'm happy to pull those funds back." Quinn grinned at me. "I'm not a hundred percent sure, but I think I can convince Addie to come with me, too."

I curled my fingers around his elbow. "I would."

Lucy glared at me. "Fine. But if I find out you're not who you say you are, you're going to regret it."

"I'll take my chances," Quinn said dryly. He stepped around her, gently tugging me along. We didn't say a word to each other until we were inside the car and out of the parking lot.

"I thought for sure she'd peg you as law enforcement," I said, once my heart stopped pounding.

"Nah. Someone like Lucy never expects to get busted. She's more worried about a competitor taking her down from the inside. I noticed she's been watching me closely lately, but I figured it was because I showed no interest in anyone else."

"Just like she accused you of."

"If I don't know who's real and who's fake, there's no way to sort through the truth."

"And you knew I was a real member."

"You're the most genuine out of everyone there."

I glanced at him. "Thanks, I think?"

"It's a compliment, but I'll deny it if you tell anyone else."

We drove to the parking lot location Hardy had texted and pulled in beside his vehicle. I scrambled out of the vehicle and into Hardy's, launching myself at him across the center console.

He grunted when I slammed into him, curling me into a tight hug. "That's a nice greeting," he murmured against my hair.

"This case is dumb," I muttered. "Dating is dumb. Quinn's dumb, too."

"I heard that," Quinn said as he opened the back passenger door.

"Still true."

Hardy's chest vibrated with amusement. "It's almost over. We only have to do this for a little while longer."

Quinn shut the door. "I hope you brought coffee."

I untangled myself from my fiancé and put my seatbelt on.

"There's a drink container inside the cooler on the floorboard. Want to pass them up?"

Quinn rummaged around before passing two coffees to us. I took a sip and shuddered. Still hot.

"You're the best," I said.

Quinn echoed the sentiment.

"Let's go," Hardy said, as he started the car. "Tonight, we'll close out Derek's case. If we can figure out how he's tied into the dating company, maybe we can close out the other one before the end of the week."

I crossed my fingers and whispered a little prayer.

TWENTY-SEVEN

I snapped my fingers. "Almost forgot. Lucy accused Quinn of being a spy for Markie." It had taken me a while to place the name. "She's the friend who recommended Harper for the service."

"Interesting," Hardy murmured. "You haven't seen this woman since?"

"I don't know what she looks like," I admitted. "Harper could identify her. I'll ask if she has a picture."

Quinn chimed in from the back. "She also thought I was working for another dating company. Divine something."

Hardy sighed. "This is a mess."

I sent a message to Harper. She responded right away.

No pictures. I could point her out to you.

"Harper doesn't have a picture." I sighed. "Also, Lucy said Speed Dating for Love is leaving within the week."

"Time is running out," Hardy remarked. "If we don't

find out who did this before they leave, you and I will be off the case."

Quinn stretched. "As terrible as that would be," he said dryly, "I'd hate to bring anyone new to the fold."

"You're going to miss us terribly," I said. "It's okay if you're too manly to admit it."

Hardy's teeth flashed white in the dim light. He pulled into a parking spot and turned off the vehicle. We were at a hotel two towns over.

"Not an apartment this time?" I asked.

"Nope. A hotel has more anonymity. Seems like Derek is stepping up his game."

I shuddered. "Can you imagine being married to someone like that?"

"Not even a little," Hardy said.

"Straight infidelity case?" Quinn inquired from the back.

"Mostly," Hardy said. "He's involved with Lucy, but we aren't sure if it's personal or if he's a member or a partner in the business."

"The money," Quinn remembered. "What bar was this again?"

I told him the name.

"Have you been back?"

I groaned. "We might be private investigators, but neither of us like this current life we've been thrust into."

Quinn snickered. "Not into the bar scene?"

"Or the dating scene, or the drink scene, or the constant nights of staying up past eleven," I said.

"I hear you. Not that I have much of a choice."

Hardy glanced at him in the rearview, his expression unreadable. "You ever thought of settling into a normal job?"

"Like what?" Quinn took his seatbelt off and stretched out.

"Private investigator."

My attention snapped to Hardy before I turned to watch Quinn.

"Short on manpower?" Quinn asked, with an amused curve to his lips.

"We're doing fine. I'm just saying sometimes a town grows on you, and it's difficult to leave."

Quinn looked away, his jaw tightening. "Once the speed-daters leave, I'll be reassigned somewhere else. It's not that easy to leave a career."

"How long have you been an agent?" I asked.

"Twenty years," he answered.

Hardy blew out a low whistle. "Thinking of retiring any time soon?"

"What would I do?" Quinn asked. "Stay at home alone, mourning my old life?" He shrugged. "This keeps me busy. I travel, see new things, meet new people."

"Do you?" Hardy asked, the question hinting at more than one meaning.

Quinn huffed. "You asking me to come here and work with you?"

Hardy's lips twisted. "I'm saying we're here if you want to stick around. We could use your skills. If you think there's nothing here for you, I'll wish you well when it's time to leave."

Hardy might be even more softhearted than I was. He saw the same deep well of grief in Quinn that I did. But he also saw how he behaved around Harper.

And I noticed how Harper behaved around Quinn. This had the potential to blow up in our faces, and while I was a little annoyed with Hardy not running this by me, the agent had grown on me. Like a barnacle, but still...he wasn't a bad sort. His loneliness was a palpable thing.

Maybe Quinn just needed people.

Us.

Maybe he just needed us. For a little while.

I reached over and squeezed Hardy's hand to let him know we were okay.

A long silence fell in the car.

"Yeah, alright," Quinn said from the back. "I'll think about it."

I ducked my head to hide my smile.

We waited a good two hours before we spotted Derek. This time, his arm was slung around a much younger blonde, this one with straight hair. He spun her around and kissed her before smacking her rear end.

"Gross," I whispered.

They finally separated and got into a pickup truck. Hardy waited until they'd pulled out of the parking lot and were a little way down the road before he started the vehicle and pulled out behind them.

"What do you want to bet they're going back to the same bar?" Quinn asked from the back.

"Nooooo," I moaned. "That's it. I quit."

Hardy snorted. "Even if it means Harper goes to jail?"

"You're playing dirty pool," I growled. "Can I stay in the car?"

"Nope," Quinn said cheerfully. "A single woman can gather a ton more information than two dudes in suits walking in. You're already dressed for a night out. You'll blend in better. Just make sure Derek doesn't see you."

"I don't think he'd recognize me if he did. I wasn't blonde last time." I glanced down at myself. "I wasn't anything like this, actually." I couldn't wait to put on joggers when I got home. Wearing heels all the time was for the birds.

"Do I have to?" I whined.

Hardy squeezed my fingers. "You don't."

Quinn barked a protest.

"But," he said, shooting a warning glare at Quinn, "it would be helpful if you did. Quinn is right. You'll be able to get a lot closer."

Quinn's prediction was right. Derek headed straight to the same bar and strutted in with the new blonde, a chubby arm slung around the woman's small waist.

"What is it these women see in him?" I murmured.

"Money," Hardy and Quinn said at the same time.

"Everything always comes back to money. Predictable." I waited until they were inside and slid out of the vehicle, shrugging off my coat and leaving it on the front seat. The chilly air hit me, and I shivered. "I'll be back as soon as I can."

"Half an hour," Hardy said. "If I don't hear from you before then, I'm coming in to find you."

I blew a kiss at him and headed inside.

The bar was just as busy tonight as it was when we'd been here. I merged into a sea of bodies, keeping my eyes peeled for Derek.

"Hey baby," someone said in my ear.

"No," I snapped and kept moving.

"You here alone?" someone else asked.

"No," I snapped again.

By the time I'd made a circle around the room, I realized the saying that blondes had more fun was only partly true. There were certainly more opportunities for fun than there'd ever been when I was a brunette, but this temporary blonde was uninterested in every single invitation.

There. Derek and the woman occupied a small, round table toward the back. Their heads were close together as they spoke. He'd draped a lazy arm over her shoulders and nuzzled her ear every once in a while.

I found a post and stood against it, pulling my cellphone up and pretending to take a selfie. I fluffed my hair and made a kissy face while snapping pictures of them. Music boomed around me, the bass matching the beat of my heart.

I double-checked to ensure everything was in focus, then tucked my phone back into my purse. But just as I was about to leave, Lucy strode right up to their table and snagged a seat. I scrambled for my phone again, changing positions to get a closer look.

This time, Derek looked taken by surprise. Lucy's smile was that of a cat who ate the canary. She flicked her fingers at the girl, who said something heated. Derek whispered something in her ear, and she snatched her purse and stalked away.

I snapped several pictures of them before ducking back into the crowd to follow the blonde.

As soon as I entered the bathroom, the sound of sobbing led me to the third stall where the woman sat on the toilet seat with her knees drawn up. She hadn't closed the door, so I gently pushed it open, trying not to show how grossed out I was. I'd never been so emotional that I forgot exactly how disgusting public restrooms were.

"Are you okay?" I asked gently.

She lifted her head, mascara leaving streaked dirty trails down her cheeks. "Who are you?"

I gave her a fake name just in case she talked to Derek later. "Sienna. I heard you when I came in. Are you here with someone?"

She sniffed. "I was. He ditched me for some old chick. Told me to go away like I was a stray cat or something."

"I'm sorry to hear that. Were you dating long?"

The woman wiped her nose with her arm. "A few months."

Oh boy. "I'm really sorry to hear that. Men are the worst, aren't they?"

A watery laugh escaped her. "The absolute worst. He

said we were going to get married and travel to the islands in a few months. Said he was coming into a ton of money."

"Oh?" I leaned against the stall door. "Did he have a rich uncle die?"

She laughed again. "You're funny, you know that?"

I shrugged. "Just have experience with terrible men." Not really, but she didn't need to know that.

"He said some company owed him big time—he had evidence that would blow the thing wide open, and they were paying him to keep his mouth shut."

This girl was a walking gossip factory. My eyes widened. "Wow. Are we talking millions or what? Lucky girl. You could buy a yacht!"

She grinned. "He never said. Only told me he'd never have to worry about money again."

Interesting. "Well, I'm glad you're okay. I can walk you out if you're leaving. I didn't catch your name, by the way."

"Hannah." Her eyes glittered with anger. "I'm not leaving yet. He thinks he can just kick me to the curb." She rose from the toilet and adjusted her skirt. "I'll show him."

And that was my cue to leave. "Hope you get that yacht," I called as I headed out.

TWENTY-EIGHT

Lucy and Derek were still deep in conversation when I passed by on my way out. I kept my face turned away and merged seamlessly into the crowd. Once I made it outside, I let out a relieved breath and hurried to the car, grabbing my coat and placing it over my knees as I sat down.

"Lots to tell you. Let's get out of here."

Without a word, Hardy pulled away and got us back onto the road.

"You found something," Quinn said.

"Lucy showed up."

Hardy's hands tightened on the steering wheel. "Tell us everything."

When I finished, Quinn swore. "I may need to put Derek on the bureau's radar. It's possible he knows who killed Aaron."

"Provided that's the evidence he's talking about," Hardy added.

"We're still going to chat with those women tomorrow?" I asked, struggling to contain my yawn.

"I'm coming with you," Quinn said. "I'll tell my partner later."

I let my head fall back against the headrest. "How did my life become a buddy comedy?"

"We'll drop you back at your car. Grab a bag and come back to the house. You can sleep on the couch. We're leaving at first light." Hardy flipped the heater to high when he noticed me still shivering.

Quinn bumped the top of my headrest. "Road trip!" he sang.

Hardy's small smile warmed my heart. I think my future husband had somehow managed to find his BFF in this debacle.

THE NEXT MORNING came way too early. Before I could even say good morning, Hardy pressed a travel mug of coffee in my hand.

"Bless you," I croaked.

Hardy winked. He looked sinfully handsome this morning. Light-wash jeans, a collared shirt underneath a pullover sweater, and slip-on loafers. He hadn't shaved this morning, leaving an enticing five o'clock shadow dusting his cheeks and chin.

Quinn wore his usual wardrobe of slacks and collared shirt, though he'd forgone the tie this time.

"You don't have any jeans?" I asked.

Quinn blinked and looked down at himself. "I didn't bring any, no. I only wear jeans when I'm off duty."

"You are off duty."

He shook his head. "We're going to question people. I need to dress the part."

"Weirdo." I sipped my coffee and wandered over to the couch. Pulling the blanket over my lap, I glared at both men. "Let me get half of this down the pipe, and I'll get dressed."

Quinn looked at Hardy. "Is that why you set the clocks ahead?"

I gasped with outrage.

"Yup. She moves at the speed of a sloth this early in the morning."

"Hardy! You made me get up early?"

He chuckled and walked over to press a kiss to my lips. "Just this once. I promise."

"You owe me so big," I muttered. "So big, mister."

"I know." He kissed me again. "I'll make it up to you."

Quinn scoffed. "Get a room."

"We have one," I growled. "This is our house, interloper."

Quinn laughed. "You're right. She is a bear in the morning."

I threw a pillow at him, which he dodged with ease.

Thirty minutes later, I was changed and had topped my coffee up. My duffle sat by the front door. Poppy rested in her carrier, blinking at us. Quinn and Hardy sat on the barstools, watching me flit around the house while I tried to figure out what I'd forgotten.

Probably nothing, but it didn't stop me from double-checking everything and retracing my steps.

When I was at last satisfied, I tied my hair back and grabbed my mug. "Ready?"

Quinn rolled his eyes. "We've been ready, Dakota."

"Just for that, I'm going to play crime podcasts all the way there."

We glared at each other long enough for Hardy to groan. "Children, can we go now?"

Quinn rose. I walked past him, grabbing my duffel and Poppy's carrier. "Shotgun!" I called.

"Does she have to come?" he whined to Hardy.

My fiancé's exasperated sigh followed me out.

THE FIRST HOUSE was a pretty Craftsman style with a freshly stained porch. Baskets and planters crowded the front door, all blooming with a riot of color. I knocked on the door and stepped back. Hardy and Quinn stood in the front yard.

Showing up unannounced wasn't the same as it used to be. Fewer people than ever actually answered the door, and one of the best ways to put them at ease was to step away from the front door so they'd open it up enough to talk.

Since we were visiting a female, Hardy and Quinn stayed far enough away so she wouldn't feel intimidated by their presence.

A pretty woman somewhere in her mid-thirties answered the door. She left the screen door closed and stared at me curiously.

"Hi, I'm Dakota," I greeted. "Are you familiar with Speed Dating for Love?" Her face shuttered, but she nodded. I introduced us. "This is my fiancé, Hardy, and Quinn Bryant, with the FBI."

"FBI?" she said faintly.

Quinn flashed his badge.

The woman sighed. "I'm Anna."

"Hardy and I are private investigators. We'd like to speak to you about Aaron Parker."

Her brow furrowed. "Aaron Parker? I'm afraid I don't know who that is."

I turned to look at Hardy. He came up the steps with his cell held out. "This man. Do you know him?"

Her lips pressed together. "Max." She blew out a breath. "I'm not surprised you thought his name was Aaron."

"He's also known as Michael O'Connor," Quinn said, coming up beside Hardy.

Anna held the door open. "Might as well come in."

Her house was cheery and borderline cluttered with colorful knick-knacks. A Russian Blue cat blinked sleepily at us from its perch on the back of the couch. "Aww." I gave it a scratch under the chin. "Mine is in her hammock in the car."

"You brought your cat?" Anna asked, giving me a strange look.

"She loves to travel," I said sheepishly.

"Want to bring her in? Sassy is friendly."

"I'd love to!" I said.

"I'll grab her," Hardy said. He turned back toward the car.

"Tea?" Anna offered.

"I'd love a cup, ma'am," Quinn said.

Hardy came back holding Poppy, who yowled loudly when she spotted me.

Anna gasped. "A Persian! She's lovely!" She made a clicking noise with her tongue and let Poppy smell her before she scratched Poppy behind the ears. "May I?"

"Sure." I handed Poppy over and let Anna introduce her to Sassy.

A moment later, Sassy and Poppy were sitting next to each other on the couch, staring at us judgmentally.

"Well," Anna said with a laugh. "Looks like Sassy made a friend." She gestured for us to head into the living room. We settled into a half circle and waited for Anna to come back in with a tray.

When we each held a steaming mug, Anna settled onto a pretty, floral-patterned chair. "What would you like to know?"

Quinn leaned forward, a notebook and pen in his hand. "If you'd start at the beginning, we'd appreciate it.

Any small thing you might dismiss as irrelevant, please tell us anyway. Hardy and Dakota are private investigators working on the case for a friend, and I am working in conjunction with them because our interests have aligned."

Anna tilted her head in curiosity, studying us with a gleam of sharp intellect. "Is Max..." Her voice trailed off.

"He was murdered a short time ago," Quinn said.

Anna closed her eyes. She let out a slow breath before a beautiful smile crossed her face. "Karma," she whispered. "I knew it was only a matter of time."

I ducked my head to hide a smile. None of us expected her to be sad about the guy's demise, but I don't think any of us expected happiness either.

When she spoke, her words were hesitant at first. Anna was already a soft-spoken woman, but by the time she finished, her voice trembled with rage.

"How much did he take from you?" Hardy asked.

"Fifty thousand," Anna said. "My life savings."

I inhaled sharply. Anna sent me a sad smile. "Yes. It didn't happen all at once. He was smart like that. It happened slowly. An ask here, an ask there. A business opportunity. A broken-down car. A plane ticket." Her eyes tightened. "I had no idea how far gone I was until I woke up one morning and he'd slipped away like a thief in the night."

"Did he leave a letter?" Quinn asked.

"No. Nothing like that. He took his car and the new clothes I bought him, and when I tried to pull the money back, I realized he'd withdrawn the rest of my savings and closed the account." A tear slipped down her face. "Did you know that many banks won't allow you to remove your name from an account without the permission of both signers, but they allow you to drain it and close it without it?" She shook her head. "Of all the dumb policies..." A harsh laugh escaped her. "By the time I figured out what he'd done, he was long gone, and I didn't even have a real name to track him down by."

We stayed a little while longer. Quinn took a ton of notes, but it was obvious Anna wasn't our killer. When we were ready to go, we had to hunt Poppy down, who loudly yowled her displeasure about leaving her new friend.

Anna tsked and scratched Poppy on the head. "Maybe soon you can come back and visit."

Poppy booped Anna on the forehead making her laugh.

Soon enough we were on the road, headed to the second house, where we heard a similar story, and then the third, where again, the man had managed to thoroughly love-bomb and fleece yet another victim. By the end of the day, I wanted to swear off all men and become a hermit in the woods.

Even Quinn and Hardy had gotten grim after the third sad tale.

"Is there any way they can get their money back?" I asked, as we headed to the hotel for the evening.

"More than likely not," Quinn answered. "They can sue the man's estate, but it's possible he won't have much."

"Is there any way you can check?" Hardy asked.

Quinn's eyes narrowed. "I might be able to find out."

Hardy and I locked eyes. We were definitely going to hint to these women about suing if we found out Michael had a cent to his name. Even if Quinn couldn't find anything out, we might still suggest it.

"How about ordering a pizza and settling in for the night?" Hardy asked.

"Good with me," I said.

Quinn grunted in agreement. "One more to go tomorrow?"

"Yep. Next town over," Hardy said. "We should be back home by lunch tomorrow."

"Thank goodness." Once this was over, I didn't plan to get out of my pajamas for an entire week.

Poppy hopped into my arms when we stopped. I kissed her on her fuzzy head and got out of the car. She was a little livelier today than she'd been these last several days, and I was hopeful she'd just fallen into a temporary feline depression.

The hotel suite was separated into two sleeping areas on opposite sides of the room with a kitchen and living room between them. I carried Poppy into the room and let her explore to her heart's content while I went back into the kitchen and made a pot of coffee.

Quinn and Hardy came in with the rest of the luggage. When everything was put where it belonged, for tonight at least, we all sank into a seat and went quiet.

I pulled up the local food delivery app and scrolled. "If

we don't want pizza, there's a wing place with good reviews, and a place that has tacos."

"Don't care," Quinn said as he kicked off his shoes.

"Your choice, Dakota," Hardy said.

"How about pizza and wings?" I said.

"Score." Quinn weakly punched his fist in the air.

Junk food and couch time. A girl's best friend.

TWENTY-NINE

The next woman's house sat on the top of a small hill, down a bumpy road that caused Poppy to loudly yowl her displeasure. She hopped out of her hammock and into my arms, clinging to my jacket as Hardy tried to navigate the road as best he could.

The potholes were so bad we might need new shocks on the vehicle when we got out of here.

I held Poppy close, doing my best to shield her from the worst of it. When we finally made it up the long drive, a bedraggled house loomed before us. It wasn't in a complete state of disrepair. Not yet, at least, but it was in dire need of a new porch and paint.

"Are you sure someone lives here?" Quinn asked from the back.

"No," Hardy answered. "The book had a first initial and address, but has no dates listed. We're flying by the seat of our pants with this."

"Good to know," Quinn said.

Hardy and I ignored the sarcasm.

I carried Poppy with me, carefully navigating the rotten boards on the porch, and knocked on the door. Poppy had settled down, content in my arms, and while it was probably weird to knock on someone's door holding a cat, it wasn't the weirdest thing I'd ever done in my life, so I went with it. I'd put her back in the car if I needed to, though I found Poppy was a door opener for most people.

No one answered. Hardy stood beside me, wearing a thunderous frown.

"What's wrong?" I whispered.

He gave a sharp shake of his head and took a step to the side, leaning down to peer through one of the dirty windows.

A loud creak inside the house sent my heartbeat ratcheting up.

I glanced at Quinn. His hand hovered over the butt of his gun. He and Hardy looked at each other, some silent conversation I wasn't privy to happening between them.

I knocked again. Quinn motioned with his hand. Hardy nodded and hopped off the side of the porch and went around the house.

"Is everything okay?"

Quinn's lips tightened. "Just follow my lead," he said.

As if that was a completely innocuous and not at all frightening thing to say while I stood on a stranger's porch completely vulnerable.

"Hello?" I called. "My name is Dakota. I'd like to talk

to you about an incident a few years ago." I held my cat up to the peephole. "And this is Poppy. She's friendly."

Quinn snorted softly and rolled his eyes.

"Hey," I hissed. "Most people like cats. Shove it, Columbo."

A flash of teeth appeared on his face, there and gone in an instant. Glad I was so amusing.

Hardy came around the other side of the house and shook his head.

"Try one more time," Hardy said quietly. "If no one answers, we're leaving."

I knocked again. Another loud creak, then a shift of a curtain in a different window. Someone was definitely home, and they didn't want to talk to us.

Hardy fished a business card from his wallet, opened the screen door, and tucked it into the top of the doorknob. "Let's go," he whispered.

Poppy meowed loudly and squirmed to get out of my arms. "We're leaving," I whispered.

She meowed again and made an impossible spine-bending motion that would have put me in traction for a week, leaping from my arms in one lithe move.

"Poppy," I hissed.

The dang cat sped off like a rocket across the porch and around the side of the house.

Quinn stared at the place where she was just a second ago and frowned. "Does she always do that?"

"More often than I'd like," I muttered.

Sighing, I carefully picked my way off the porch and

went around the house, careful to watch my step. Debris littered the yard. Children's toys and tools, gardening supplies, and empty pots. Whoever lived here had obviously given up or just plain didn't care about appearances.

I spotted a familiar orange fur coat several feet ahead, sitting on top of a pile of what looked to be trash.

Hardy came up beside me and took my elbow. "Think it's something?"

I chuckled. "It's always something with Poppy, isn't it?"

Quinn trailed behind, eyes scanning in all directions. He never took his hand off the butt of his gun.

When we got closer, Hardy held up a hand to stop me. "Stay here. There could be snakes or other unpleasant surprises."

"Isn't it too cold for them?" Quinn asked.

"Probably, but they don't actually hibernate. They'll be slower, which will work in our favor, but I'd rather not find one at all." Hardy moved closer and peered down at Poppy. She moved to the side and swatted something on the ground.

Quinn's eyes narrowed. "Is your cat...weird?"

"Very," I said. "Sometimes she does things that make me feel like she's a human soul trapped in a feline body."

Hardy crouched down and took a picture of whatever had Poppy so interested.

"What is it?" I asked.

"Just a sign." Hardy shook his head and rose. "I don't understand what she's trying to tell us."

"Come on, Poppy," I called.

She gave me a look and batted the sign again.

"Hardy has it," I assured her. "We don't know what it means, but he took a picture. We'll find out."

"And you talk to her about cases." Quinn shook his head. "I've seen everything."

Poppy hopped off the pile and strutted past Quinn, showing him her butt.

I grinned and held out my arms for her. In one smooth leap, she landed on me. "Good girl." I kissed her on top of the head and headed back to the car.

When we were off that awful road, Hardy fished his cell out. "Look at the picture and tell me if it rings a bell."

I opened his camera roll, smiled when I saw candid photos of me I didn't realize he'd taken, and pulled up the photo of the pile. An old, dirty sign that said *Stone Realty* lay face up.

The name sounded familiar, but I couldn't remember where I'd heard it from. I showed Quinn the sign, but he shook his head.

"No idea. I also didn't realize cats could read."

I covered Poppy's ears. "You'll hurt her feelings."

Quinn laughed. "You two are the strangest people I've ever met, and that's saying a lot."

Hardy's gaze flicked to Quinn. "I'd consider us pretty normal." His lips twisted. "Except for the cat."

My cell dinged with a text.

Markie dropped by unexpectedly. Things are a little weird. Think you can stop by?

"How far are we away from Silverwood?" I asked Hardy.

He glanced at the map on his phone. "Forty-five minutes."

I winced. "Markie showed up at Harper's place."

I didn't need to tell Hardy twice. He hit the gas, and soon we were flying toward home.

THIRTY

"Park down the block," I urged, as I touched up the last of my Addie makeup and fluffed the blonde wig I was beginning to loathe.

"Good idea," Quinn said. "I'll come with you."

"I'll go with her. You go around to the back of the house and stay hidden until we need you."

Quinn barked a laugh. "Forgot myself for a second. Alright." He eyed Hardy. "Carrying a gun?"

"I am."

"Good."

The atmosphere had shifted into a tense sort of silence. Poppy shivered in my arms. "Stay in the car," I whispered to the cat.

Hardy pulled up to the curb three houses down from Harper's. I handed Poppy to Hardy and got out, hurrying to the house.

Harper answered the door after knocking twice, wearing a wide, fake smile. Her eyes were full of fear.

"Oh my gosh! What a lovely surprise," she gushed, as she pulled me inside. "Come in! There's someone I want you to meet."

Harper shut the door behind us and clamped her fingers so tightly around my arm that it hurt.

A woman sat on the couch watching us. My heart sank to my toes. I knew her.

Markie was the same woman we'd caught with Derek on our first surveillance. She had thankfully never spotted us, something that could only work in our favor now.

"Hello," I said politely, my heartbeat skittering like a frightened rabbit.

She gave me a thin smile.

"I'm Addie."

"Markie."

Harper led me into the living room. I sat on a chair as far away from Markie as I could get.

"Coffee or tea?" Harper offered, a strained smile on her lips.

"Coffee would be wonderful." Just in case I needed to defend myself. The hotter the better.

Harper scurried to the kitchen. Her house had an open floor plan, so I could keep an eye on her the entire time, but that also meant Markie could see her. She must have somehow sneaked that text message to me without Markie knowing.

"So," I said, smiling at the woman I was beginning to suspect of being a murderer, "how do you know Harper?"

She waved a hand. "Oh, here and there, you know." Exactly the sort of answer I'd expect.

"She said you recommended her for that wonderful speed-dating place. I have to admit, I wasn't sure what to think when she told me about it, especially after that dreadful business with Aaron, but Harper has such a good attitude about life, you know? Even though it didn't work out for her, she thought it might for me!"

"You've been to an event?" Markie asked, perking up a little at the subject of dating.

"Three now!" I laughed self-deprecatingly. "And I'm dating a very nice man."

Harper set our mugs down.

"That's good news," Markie said.

"It really is," I said with a sigh. "How did you stumble onto that membership?"

Markie's smile faded. "A friend of a friend."

"Oh? Did it work out for you?"

Markie grabbed her purse and rose. "I'm sorry, Harper. I just remembered an appointment I have. Thanks so much for the coffee, but I need to run."

Harper could barely hide the relief on her face. "Oh no. I'm sorry to hear that."

They walked to the door. "I'll stop back by soon," Markie said, as she hurried outside.

Harper sank against the door as soon as she shut it.

"Hardy and Quinn are outside," I said, as I shot both of them a text letting them know the coast was clear.

She opened the door again to let them in.

Quinn gently gripped her upper arm. "Are you okay?" he said earnestly. "Why are you back in your house? Shouldn't you still be at your parents'?"

"Whoa," I said, my eyes darting back and forth between them. "Intense much, Quinn?"

He shot me a dark look.

Harper pulled away. "Because this is my house, and I don't want to hide like a rat!"

Hardy's eyes widened a hair as he made a beeline for me.

"What did Markie say?" I asked, breaking up the tension between them. None of our business.

"She was asking a lot of questions about you and Quinn, actually."

My heart skipped a beat. "What kind of questions?"

"Where I knew you from. If I knew Quinn. If I'd heard anything about Aaron." Harper looked down at her feet. "She was starting to scare me, so I hurried to the bathroom and sent that text."

"Good call." I rose and took Hardy's hand. "As much as I hate to say this, I think you should come home with us. Just for the night."

Harper groaned.

"One night," I cajoled. "I have a feeling things are going to end quickly."

She sighed. "Fine. I'll grab a bag." Harper disappeared

into the back of the house. I waited until her bedroom door shut before I addressed the elephant in the room.

"Are you out of your mind?" I hissed at Quinn.

His eyes widened. "What?"

"Why are you being all macho dude to her? You aren't even dating!"

Quinn blinked a few times, brow furrowing. "I—I don't know."

"Well cut it out," I snapped. "It's obvious you like her, but you're going to blow any potential right out of the water if you don't treat her like an adult."

Quinn's lips thinned, and he stalked out of the house, slamming the door behind him.

"You really have a way with people," Hardy quipped.

"Bluuuuurgh," I groaned, pinching the space between my eyebrows.

WE DROPPED Poppy and Quinn off and headed to meet with Paige. She'd chosen the same place we'd met for the first time. I waved when I spotted her in a booth at the back and made a beeline toward her.

I scooted in first, followed by Hardy. A server hurried over and took our drink order. Paige had already ordered a cappuccino and a muffin, but I wasn't hungry.

"Tell me you have news," Paige said when the server left.

Hardy nodded. "Another woman. I'll e-mail you all the pictures when I return to the office."

Paige frowned. "You've never seen the first woman again?"

On the way over, Hardy and I agreed not to say a word about Markie as it related to our case. Something was off about the entire thing, and until I knew how all the puzzle pieces fit, I thought it appropriate we kept everything separate. Even though I knew Derek was somehow involved in the dating company, Paige had hired us to investigate his infidelity.

Hardy readily agreed and voiced the same suspicion I had about Paige. She seemed innocent and only concerned about her husband, but I'd done this long enough to realize that maybe we didn't have all the information.

"No. We've never spotted her on a date with your husband again." True. Sort of.

"Who was the second woman?"

I lied about the bathroom conversation, too. "I never got close enough to ask her any questions. He dismissed her a little while into their date because another woman came up to him for a chat."

Interest sparked in her eyes. "Oh? Who was she?"

"No idea, ma'am. Though their relationship didn't seem personal."

"Ah." Paige nodded and dug through her purse, pulling out a thick white envelope. She pushed it across the table. "For services rendered."

Hardy and I had also discussed the matter of payment. We both decided to take the woman's money even if she were involved in Aaron's death, simply because we'd expended a ton of time and effort and had proven what she wanted. Their divorce or anything following was none of our business.

But something nagged at me. "I'm afraid I've misplaced your business card. Do you have another?"

"Of course!" She handed me another one, and I passed it to Hardy as soon as I skimmed it.

Another piece of the puzzle locked into place.

Hardy went still. Good. He'd noticed it, too.

The server brought our coffees over. We made small talk for a little while until we made our excuses to leave. I tucked the envelope into my purse, and we hurried outside.

Neither of us spoke until we were in the car on the way back to the office.

"Stone Realty," Hardy growled.

"Yup." The sign Poppy had pointed out was the name of the business that Paige owned.

The woman was involved in this up to her eyeballs.

"We need Quinn's help. I don't have the same access I used to have with the department."

I reached over and took his hand. "We're almost there."

Hardy huffed a laugh. "Thank goodness."

THIRTY-ONE

Quinn wasted no time. Right after I called the bookstore to make sure everything was okay, I changed into lounge clothes, made a new pot of coffee, and thawed out some chicken for dinner.

I was in the mood for comfort food.

Harper texted saying she was on her way over, so I took an extra pack of chicken out of the freezer just in case.

Hardy kissed me and headed out to pick Izzy up. We'd both missed her terribly and couldn't wait to see her.

Which left me and Quinn at the house. This was the first time I'd ever been truly alone with him.

"Don't even say it," he growled, when I set a steaming cup of coffee in front of him.

I laughed. "She's a wonderful person," was all I said.

He grunted and kept staring at his laptop screen.

I settled in and picked up the newest thriller I'd gotten

in at the store. It wasn't as good as Daniel's new book, but it was good enough to keep me turning pages.

A knock on the door jerked me away some minutes later. Harper stood there, holding a small backpack. She'd changed into leggings, boots, and a long tunic shirt with a sweater coat over it. Her hair was tied up in a messy bun atop her head, and she'd taken her makeup off, revealing a pretty, but tired face.

I held my arms out. Harper stepped into them, drew in a ragged breath, and started to cry.

Quinn stood up and closed the door behind us, watching Harper and me but not interfering. I took the poor woman to the kitchen, sat her down, and made her a cup of coffee, adding a healthy dash of Bailey's to it.

She smiled weakly. "Thanks."

Quinn sat back down and kept typing, wisely keeping his mouth shut.

"Izzy will be home in a little while," I said.

Harper's face brightened. "She really is the best."

"I know. I can't wait to be her stepmom."

We smiled at each other, the stress of the last several days fading away as the future opened up.

"You're going to be married soon," Harper said.

"Crazy, right?"

She gave me a strange smile. "Not at all. Overdue. I hoped you'd work it out."

Quinn stood up and carried his laptop over to the dining table. "I have something."

"Let's wait for Hardy. He won't be gone long."

Less than ten minutes later, an exuberant Izzy barreled through the door. She headed straight for me and buried her head in my stomach as she wrapped her arms around my hips.

"Hey, sweetie." I ruffled her hair and hugged her back.

She let go and reached for Harper, who dragged her into a tight hug.

When Izzy spotted Quinn, she waved. "Hey, Mr. Quinn."

"Hi, Izzy." Quinn smiled. He motioned for Hardy to come over.

Harper rose from her chair. "Want to show me your room, Izzy?"

I smiled gratefully at her. "Baked chicken with cream sauce tonight for dinner. Want to pick the veggie before you show Auntie Harper?"

Izzy squinted her eyes as she thought about it. "Potatoes."

"Alright. How about a green, too?"

"Broccoli!"

"Done."

She grinned and bounded away, dragging Harper to the back.

Quinn waited until they were out of earshot. "Stone Realty leased a house to an untraceable company about six months ago. There's no way to tell who was in there without the full name."

Hardy pulled the notebook out.

"What were the initials of the last person we visited?"

He skimmed the page. "M. E."

"Markie?" I asked.

Hardy's expression tightened. "She couldn't have been in the house when we were there because she was at Harper's."

"Maybe she has kids?" I asked.

"Or a husband," Quinn added.

Hardy groaned. "I think we need to do one more round of surveillance."

"Not tonight. We're having a nice dinner first and visiting with Izzy." I needed a good night's sleep.

"Agreed," Quinn said, which surprised the heck out of me.

I peered at Hardy. He blew out a breath. "You're right. Let's take tonight as a rest day and finish things up tomorrow."

AS MOST PLANS WENT, it didn't quite work out that way. Earlier in the day, Quinn had sent someone to follow Paige. The agent was reporting back periodically, but there was nothing of interest until Paige got into her vehicle and headed straight for Silverwood. Thankfully, we'd eaten a good dinner, and it was late enough that Izzy was already tucked into bed.

Harper held up her phone and frowned. "Markie just texted me. She wants to meet in an hour."

Hardy and I gave each other a meaningful look. Maybe we could end this tonight. It couldn't be a coincidence that

Paige was headed our way and Markie wanted to meet up with Harper.

"I'll call Mom," I said. "Someone has to stay with Izzy, and we're going to need all hands on deck for this."

"I'll put backup on hold," Quinn said, already reaching for his phone.

Mom arrived within twenty minutes. "Be careful," she urged. "This sounds dangerous."

I gave her a hug. "This time I have a lot more backup than usual."

Mom eyed Quinn. "You're a handsome devil, aren't you?"

Quinn cracked a laugh.

"Mom," I groaned. "Not now."

Mom sniffed. "What? I'm not blind, you know."

"Sometimes you really should try to be," I muttered.

Hardy ducked his head to hide a smile. Rolling my eyes, I grabbed a sweater. "Ready to roll?"

Everyone agreed, and we were out the door. Harper had to drive her own car. Quinn drove separately, too, leaving me and Hardy finally alone.

"This case has been wild," I said, as we drove to the meeting place. Harper had turned on her location and sent it to us in a group message. She also agreed to turn on her recorder when she met up with Markie.

We would be in the same parking lot, a safe distance away.

Quinn would be even closer, in case she needed intervention of the law enforcement kind.

"I'm exhausted," Hardy admitted.

"Should we hire more people?"

"I'm hoping Quinn comes on board."

I eyed his profile. "You think he'll leave a twenty-year career to come on board with a brand-new business?"

Hardy lifted a shoulder in a shrug. "I think Quinn is searching for something different. He needs people, and is just now realizing what that feels like again. There's a good chance he'll take us up on it."

"Huh."

Hardy couldn't suppress his grin. "You two fight like siblings."

"He annoys me greatly," I said in a prim voice.

"I couldn't tell at all," he said, deadpan.

I snorted. "Hush, you."

We made it to the hotel parking lot early. Pulling in after Markie arrived would only rouse suspicion, so we turned off the engine and waited, keeping a close eye on the road.

Harper would wait until it was closer to the time to meet before pulling in. Quinn didn't divulge where he would be, but we knew it would be close.

Silence stretched between us as we waited.

I couldn't wait until I could crawl into my bed and get a full night's sleep again.

THIRTY-TWO

Ten minutes till the top of the hour, Harper pulled in. A dark luxury car rolled in after her, followed by a blue sedan. Hardy and I ducked lower into our seats.

"Can you hear me?" Harper whispered through the line.

"We can," I said. "Good luck and be careful."

Harper's huff made me chuckle. "This is your thing," she murmured. "I just want to sell books."

"You'll get that chance as soon as this is over," I assured her.

"Keep the line open at all times," Hardy chimed in. "We got your back." He hit *mute* on the screen.

Harper exhaled a long breath and opened the vehicle door.

Markie got out of the sedan, followed by a familiar man.

"Oh no," I whispered.

Hardy stilled. "If Paige is in that other vehicle, things are going to go downhill fast," he warned.

Harper headed toward the couple, completely oblivious to Paige's presence. There was no way we could tell her, either.

I waited, trying not to hold my breath, but the anticipation was too much.

My phone vibrated. Quinn.

Who's in that other vehicle?

We think it might be Paige.

Quinn didn't respond again.

"What's going on?" Harper said.

"We know who your friend really is," Markie said.

I stiffened.

"Did you really think you could put a P.I. on our tail, and we wouldn't know?"

"Addie isn't a P.I.," Harper insisted.

"She's the only new thing to happen to our organization, and she's been asking a lot of questions," Markie snapped. "It has to be her."

Harper held up her hands. "I know nothing about it. Addie is single, and I thought she'd be a good fit."

So they didn't know me as Dakota. My shoulders sagged with relief.

A woman stepped out of the other car, her right hand hidden in the folds of her coat. She stepped around the other vehicles and came up behind Markie and Derek.

"I knew it," Paige hissed. "I knew you two were

sleeping together! I even had pictures and still didn't believe it until just now."

Derek spun around, surprise lighting his face when he saw his wife. But he quickly covered it with a sneer. "What are you going to do about it? I got enough evidence to put you away for years."

"Aaron needed to go," Paige snapped. "And you fools weren't smart enough to stay away from things until she got put away!"

Harper gasped, knowing she was the one they were talking about.

"She's still going down for it," Markie said, rolling her eyes. "They ain't got nothing on us. We only have to hold on a few more days until the company goes public."

So that's what this whole thing was about. If Speed Dating for Love was going public, they stood to make an insane amount of money.

It always came back to the money.

"Idiots," Paige hissed.

"Aaron was our best worker," Markie whined.

Harper took a step back.

"Aaron took too much. He got too cocky and too well known." Paige shook her head. "He had to die."

"You were the one to jeopardize things. Getting rid of Aaron could have waited until afterward," Markie sniped.

I glanced at Hardy. He held up his digital recorder, an extra one just in case Harper's phone disconnected or her own device didn't catch the conversation.

"Either you pay me the extra money, or I'm sending what I have to the cops," Derek said.

Paige rolled her eyes. "You have only circumstantial evidence. Nothing to put me away. I've had a P.I. tailing you for a while now. They have pictures of you meeting with Markie and Lucy and pictures of you handing money over the table to the woman." A nasty smile crossed her face. "Who do you think they're going to believe? A scorned wife like me, or a man who hasn't been able to hold down a job in years?"

Derek's lips pulled back from his teeth in a grimace. He lunged for Paige, but she gracefully dodged and held up a gun. "I'd stay right there if I were you."

Derek and Markie froze.

"I won't say a word," Markie babbled. "Just leave us alone. No one has to know you killed Aaron."

Paige scoffed. "*I* didn't kill him, you idiot. Lucy did. She was even more tired of Aaron than I was."

My jaw dropped.

At their matching looks of surprise, Paige grinned. "Consider your memberships revoked."

Harper took another step back, poised to run.

"Uh uh," Paige said. "Take one more step, and you'll regret it. You're coming with me. A handwritten confession from you should do it before you meet an untimely end by your own hand."

My nostrils flared with fury.

Are you seeing this? I wrote to Quinn.

Do not get out of your cars, he wrote back. *Stay there and wait for my signal.*

Dark shadows moved in a circular pattern around the parking lot.

I froze, not knowing what was happening until the streetlights reflected on the emblem emblazoned over their jackets.

The FBI had arrived.

A gunshot rang out.

Total chaos reigned seconds later.

HARPER SAT on the back of an ambulance, looking a little shell-shocked.

Hardy and I sat on either side of her watching a dozen agents milling around the parking lot.

Quinn approached, a genuine smile on his face.

I greeted him with, "Can we go home?"

"Not yet, I'm afraid. They're almost through with everything. Give it another half hour."

I groaned.

"Is Mr. Morgan going to make it?" Hardy asked.

Paige's shot went wild. She was aiming for Markie but hit Derek right in the upper chest.

Quinn shrugged. "Maybe. He's in critical condition." He perched on the back of the other ambulance. "I've never seen a more convoluted mess in my entire career. The dating agency will be no more in a few days. They've pulled their last fraud."

"How many people were like Harper?" I asked.

Quinn gave her a sympathetic look. "Less than twenty percent. We're trying to keep things as quiet as possible to prevent those other members from fleeing."

I glanced around the parking lot at the complete and utter chaos. "Yeah. Good luck with that."

Quinn chuckled. "We do tend to come in like a lion," he admitted.

We fell quiet for a few moments before someone called out for Quinn. "I have to run, but I wanted to come over and thank you."

"Oh? For what?" I asked.

Quinn's eyes danced with amusement. "For annoying me to death."

Hardy pressed his lips together to keep from laughing. I shot him a glare.

"Glad I could be of service," I said dryly.

"On a serious note, you and your fiancé somehow single-handedly managed to pull me out of a funk I'd been in for years." He looked away. "I haven't been the same since my wife passed away."

Harper stiffened but didn't say a word.

"I've been going through the motions, and I want to thank you for shaking things up."

"Does this mean you'll consider our offer?" Hardy asked.

A calculating gleam sparked in his eyes. "You never sent me a written offer," Quinn said.

Hardy's smile sharpened. "I think I could put something together."

Quinn turned to go. "I've thought about retiring a few times," he admitted. "Maybe once I have that offer, I'll think about it a little harder." He winked at Harper and walked away.

Harper blew out a long breath. "That man is dangerous," she murmured.

Hardy and I didn't say a word.

Dangerous for her, maybe.

EPILOGUE

Jack, the furniture maker from down the road, stood in our store frowning at our window display.

"I don't know how you managed to do it," he muttered to himself.

Harper grinned and clicked the remote control. A Halloween soundtrack kicked up, starting with The Monster Mash. I stifled my groan.

If I heard that song one more time, I might lose it.

"Technical ingenuity and creativity," Harper said solemnly, a wicked gleam in her gaze.

Jack rolled his eyes. He was a handsome devil. Tall, lean, intelligent, and quick-witted, I'd caught him stalking our window for at least a week now before he ventured inside.

He and Harper had immediately butted heads, and I stayed out of it, content to enjoy the show.

Poppy lay curled in the window display, her orange fur

matching perfectly with the spray of autumn leaves underneath her.

"The cat helps," Harper said deadpan.

"You'll lose next year," Jack said.

Harper grinned. "Maybe so." She waved the check and trophy under his nose. "But I've won this year, so I'll enjoy it for another 364 days, won't I?"

I coughed to cover my laugh. With a final glare at my partner, Jack stormed out of Tattered Pages. Poppy hissed at him as the door shut.

Harper reached over and scratched behind the cat's ears. Poppy still wasn't quite the same—a little better, but she'd lost a lot of zeal for life over the last several weeks and didn't move around nearly as much. It was worrisome.

"I think you should take her to a rescue and see how she does with another cat." Harper fussed with the leaves around Poppy before straightening.

I recalled our meeting with Sassy, the Russian blue we'd met during the case.

"You think she's lonely?" I asked.

"I do. If you've already taken her to the vet, and she's in perfect health, that would be my next step. It's perfectly normal to get lonely."

"But we have Izzy," I protested, not sure how I felt about bringing another pet into the mix.

Harper barked a surprised laugh. "Izzy is not a cat, Dakota. It's not quite the same. Just give it a try and see how she does. Let her be your guide."

I eyed Poppy. She'd tucked her head and curled into a

little apostrophe, her favorite position these days. "Alright. I guess a look couldn't hurt."

AND THAT WAS how we ended up with a two-month-old kitten named Fang...a nightmare of tooth and claw and Poppy's new best friend.

My life was so weird sometimes.

ALSO BY S.E. BABIN

A Shelf Indulgence Cozy Mystery Series

How about a ghost whisperer in a new magical town? Check out
The Psychic Cleaner series!

Psychic Cleaner

Like a little more magic with your cozies? Check out The
Magical Soapmaker Mysteries!

The Magical Soapmaker Mysteries

If you'd like a little more action and sass and don't mind some
PG-13 language, check out my Aphrodite series.

The Goddess Chronicles

Or, if you like a snarky bartender with a secretive mixed heritage,
meet Violet!

Cocktails in Hell

ABOUT THE AUTHOR

Sheryl likes cake too much and can be found hoarding it while hiding from her children in the pantry closet.

Follow her on Amazon at: https://www.amazon.com/S-E-Babin/e/B00J1J236A